THE MONSTER CATCHERS

A BAILEY BUCKLEBY STORY

THE MONSTER CATCHERS

GEORGE BREWINGTON

WITH ILLUSTRATIONS BY DAVID MILES

GODWINBOOKS

Henry Holt and Company

New York

Henry Holt and Company, *Publishers since 1866*
Henry Holt® is a registered trademark of Macmillan Publishing Group, LLC
175 Fifth Avenue, New York, NY 10010 • mackids.com

Text copyright © 2019 by George Brewington.
Illustrations copyright © 2019 by David Miles.
All rights reserved.

Library of Congress Control Number: 2018945025
ISBN 978-1-250-16578-7 (hardcover) / ISBN 978-1-250-16579-4 (ebook)

Our books may be purchased in bulk for promotional, educational, or business use. Please
contact your local bookseller or the Macmillan Corporate and Premium Sales Department
at (800) 221-7945 ext. 5442 or by email at MacmillanSpecialMarkets@macmillan.com.

First edition, 2019 / Designed by April Ward
Printed in the United States of America by LSC Communications, Harrisonburg,
Virginia.
1 3 5 7 9 10 8 6 4 2

FOR CAROLINE

THE MONSTER CATCHERS

CHAPTER ONE

PFT

BAILEY BUCKLEBY sat behind the register in the front room while his father fed the monsters in the back. A stack of Frisbees towered next to him for easy access. There had been no customers all morning, so he had been rereading his favorite book—*In the Shadow of Monsters* by monster hunter and photographer Dr. Frederick March—when four slouching tenth graders rolled through the front door with the Pacific fog. They had droopy eyes and bad ideas and gravitated to the back, feigning interest in the hermit crabs for sale. A purple curtain separated the front room from the back room, and the tenth graders knew that whatever was behind that purple curtain could make their small-town Saturday a lot more interesting.

"Hey, little seventh grader," the one without a chin said, "what's in the back?"

Shrieking pierced through the wall in perfect rhythm like an evil metronome. Mad chirping added a vicious melody. Barking as loud and deep as a bass drum boomed *ROUMP, ROUMP, ROUMP!*

"Those are dogs," Bailey said, flipping the rusty shag of hair out of his bright green eyes. He was scrawny but tough, his arms and legs well scratched from frequent falls off his skateboard and even more frequent scrapes with monsters.

"Those aren't dogs," said the one with the caveman forehead.

"Cats." Bailey shrugged, not even looking up from his book.

The sophomores didn't appreciate being put off. They were in high school after all.

"Those aren't cats." The one with chronic burping burped.

"They're cats and dogs. There's also an extra-large parrot. Are you guys going to buy something or waste my time?"

But the high schoolers didn't care about hermit crabs that made their homes out of plastic skulls. They didn't care about the handmade shark tooth necklaces, the bins of saltwater taffy, the cheap straw hats, the easy-to-break sunglasses, or the snow globes of Santa with a bare belly kicking back on the beach. Only tourists bought that stuff, and the squishy fake whale blubber, and the T-shirts that read I ATE THE WHALEFAT, because the town of Whalefat Beach, California, was famous for its barbecued whale

2

blubber sandwiches. Barbecued whale blubber sandwiches had been the town's traditional lunch for three hundred years, because legend was that a giant whale had drifted ashore there and exploded, freeing its fifty inhabitants, who feasted off the blubbery remains of their former captor while building the town with their very own hands. To tourists, and even most locals, the story was amusing but too far-fetched to be believed. Bailey's father said it was the absolute truth, and he claimed to be a direct descendant of one of those original Whalefatians, which made Bailey a Whalefatian, too.

The sophomore with three patches of fuzz on his face, who thought he had a full beard, snarled.

"Listen, Monster Boy. We know you have monsters back there, and we wanna see 'em."

"Yeah," Caveman grunted. "We wanna see 'em."

Bailey looked up at them, annoyed that they hadn't left yet. "Despite whatever rumors you idiots have heard, there are no monsters here." Then, raising his voice a pitch higher to imitate his teacher Mrs. Wood, he shooed them away. "*Run along, boys. Shoo!*"

Bailey grinned, looking back down at his book, laughing at his own joke. The teenage thugs could barely stand the insubordination. Fuzzy made one fist, then another. "Listen, *boy*. You're in seventh grade and we're in high school. You have to respect the chain of command, son!"

Pft! In less than a second, Bailey pulled a Frisbee from the stack and whipped it at the center of Fuzzy's forehead. He was momentarily stunned like a dumb cow. Bailey wasted no time, grabbed two more, and flicked his wrist. *Pft! Pft!* Two more to Fuzzy's forehead for good measure. Bailey never missed.

"Hey!" Caveman yelled. *Pft!* Grab, flick, Frisbee to his forehead.

Pft! Preemptive strike on Burper. Burper stumbled backward. *Pft!* One more to the bridge of Chinless's nose just for being ugly. Bailey's accuracy was dead-on.

The boys grabbed their foreheads in pain, paralyzed with disbelief. The Frisbee injuries would leave welts on their foreheads for all their classmates to see Monday morning—undeniable proof that they had been defeated by a seventh grader.

Just one seventh grader.

And Bailey had plenty of Frisbees left.

"I don't care what grade you guys are in. Read the sign above the door. *Buckleby and Son's Very Strange Souvenirs.* This is *my* turf. I'm the son in Buckleby and Son's, *SON!*"

"You think you can scare us off with Frisbees, little boy?" Caveman demanded.

Bailey Buckleby was a hunter and seller of monsters. He had dealt with far worse than these four adolescents. He leaned forward on the counter, his fingers crossing thoughtfully, like an adult.

"You want to know what's in the back?"

The four thugs leaned forward, gaping and slouching, and there wasn't a single twinkle of intelligence in any of their cold, dull eyes.

"You want to know what my dad and I are keeping back

there? You want to know what's back there that has *my* back?"

Bailey flipped his hair out of his eyes again and slowly reached under the register. He placed a portable baby monitor carefully on the counter, turning it to face them. The sophomores crowded together to look at the dark screen, and Bailey wondered just how long he could make these goons stare at absolutely nothing. He watched them with amusement for long stretched-out seconds until finally, with a wicked grin, he flipped the monitor switch to ON.

The screen lit up and showed them what was on the other side of the purple curtain.

Their eyes grew big.

And they ran.

CHAPTER TWO

CATCH-AND-KEEP

THE BRASS BELL above the door to Buckleby and Son's Very Strange Souvenirs dinged twice as another customer came in. He was a frightened man with thin wisps of hair wandering on the top of his head at the whim of the ocean breeze. He kept his hands in his pockets and beelined straight for Bailey at the counter.

"Yes, sir. How can I help you?"

"Hello," he whispered. "I heard from a friend of mine that you help people who have certain . . . *pest problems*."

"We don't kill roaches," Bailey said decisively, flipping a page in his book.

"Yes, I know. But you are familiar with certain strange creatures, right? How old are you?"

"Old enough."

"Eleven?"

Bailey sat up straight. "Twelve!"

"Sorry. Listen. Am I in the right place?"

"Keep talking and we'll find out."

But the shrieking and the mad chirping and the *roump, roump, roump* behind the purple curtain were sure clues to the frightened gentleman that, yes, he was.

"I have photos," he explained. He showed Bailey the photos on his phone. The first showed some strange thing that seemed to be hanging upside down as it gripped the bark of a redwood tree. The thing had long fingers, long toes, and long ears. The second photo showed the same creature reaching out for a thick rope swing, and the third showed it swinging out over a pond. Then finally, the fourth photo showed it letting go with its knees held tight to its chest in fine cannonball position.

"This is the pond on my land."

"Is that your kid jumping into your pond?" Bailey asked.

The man swallowed, horrified. "No! I don't know *what* it is. But it keeps coming back. And it *steals* things."

"What kind of things?"

"The lights off our porch and the headlights from my car."

"Hold on," Bailey said. He pressed the red intercom button. "Dad?"

No response. The intercom only amplified the shrieking, the chirping, and the *roump, roump, roump*.

"Dad? Dad?"

"Yes? What? Hello?"

"Can you come meet this customer?"

"Be there in a second. Ow! You little—"

The customer put his hand to his mouth. "What in the world is back there?"

Bailey shook his head. "I don't think you want to know."

"I don't think I want to know, either," he whispered.

Dougie Buckleby slid the purple curtain aside and entered the room. Like Bailey's, his father's hair was a rumpled rusty shag that nearly covered his bright green eyes. Unlike Bailey, Dougie was as big and hairy as a gorilla. He could barely fit through the entryway that connected the front and back rooms.

"Hello, my friend!" Bailey's father said happily and loudly. "I've seen you at the coffee shop."

"Yes. John Hanson. I live at the intersection of Ahab and Blackwater."

"Very good, John Hanson. How can I help you?"

The frightened man showed him the four photos of the strange intruder. Bailey's father took the phone from him and enlarged the photos with his fingers.

"Is that your kid?"

"No, it's not my kid," he insisted. "And it *steals* things."

"What kind of things?"

"The lights off our porch and the headlights from my car."

"I already asked him that," Bailey murmured.

"Also," Hanson whispered, leaning closer, "it scratches on our bedroom window at night if we turn the lights on.

8

My wife and I have seen its face. Bug-eyed, boils all over it, long pointy ears. It has a lot of sharp teeth—all pointed and yellow!"

His father leaned in for a closer look, squinting, but then smacked his hand down on the counter.

"Ah. No cause for concern. What you have here is a common garden gnome. They are harmless little vegetarians. Sometimes they steal chicken wire to make into necklaces. They dance in the woods and sing stupid, meaningless songs. They dig burrows and build furniture out of broken-up fence posts. Really, they're nothing more than tiny hippies. No need for alarm, but I'd suggest investing in electric fencing, which we sell and will install for you for a small additional charge. You have to shock the daylights out of garden gnomes. Only way to deal with them."

"A garden gnome?" John Hanson gasped. "Like those ceramic statues, *but alive*? Are you certain? My fence posts haven't been damaged."

Bailey looked closer. A garden gnome would have small stubby ears, small stubby fingers, and practically unseparated stubby miniature toes.

"Dad, are you sure? Maybe this is a North American tunneling goblin. *Gobelinus cuniculus*. I have a picture of it right here in my book."

His father smiled and sighed and ruffled his boy's hair. "My son is fascinated by the work of Dr. March, but really, although he's an outstanding photographer of monsters in their natural habitat, the doctor is far too sympathetic to them, as if they wouldn't eat him given the chance. We can't forget that for all their faults, humans have survived because they have kept nature's most horrifying beasts in cages. I'm sure you would agree, John."

By his confused expression, Bailey could tell this man had never even *heard* of Dr. Frederick March, even though *In the Shadow of Monsters* was the essential companion for monster hunters and traders around the world. All of Dr. March's monster photographs were accompanied by fascinating adventure stories describing how the doctor had found each monster in the wild using science and his wits, and although he quite often escaped a monster just before being eaten, he never harmed any creature he encountered, big or small. Bailey admired that, even though he felt guilty about that admiration sometimes. His father had taught him that for seven generations, Bucklebys had maintained a proud tradition of keeping their neighbors safe from monsters by whatever means necessary, which included blowing up the whale that swallowed the town's founders so many years ago. If Bailey were to believe otherwise, he knew his father would not only think he was "soft" but that he was rejecting their family's history and, even worse, rejecting *him*.

But sometimes, his father just missed important details. Bailey turned to page fifty-seven and showed him Dr. March's photograph.

"See, Dad? Look how the fingers and toes are double-jointed in both photos. Both have long and pointy ears, and the arch in the back of this goblin matches the curve of the spine of this one."

The book looked tiny in his father's giant hands. "I must admit, this photograph is quite stunning. How do you suppose the good doctor managed such close-ups? My wife, Katrina, would have been so intrigued to know goblins could be living *right here* in Whalefat Beach. She was a monster photographer herself with a keen eye for the perfect candid shot. You should see her photos of faeries in flight."

Bailey's father put the book down and wiped away the beginning of a tear before it could mature. Katrina Buckleby had been gone six and a half years and still, just the mention of her brought all his grief back to the present. John Hanson could only stare at him blankly.

"Well," his father said, forcing himself to smile. "My son appears to be quite right. Your pond intruder does resemble a North American tunneling goblin—"

"No. No, no, no!" Hanson interrupted. "I don't care what it is. I cannot have that *thing* living on my land!"

"It may not have taken up residence," Bailey's father assured him. "It may be just going for a swim. But this is quite something. At the annual Las Vegas Monster Hunters Conference, I heard rumors that goblins had been living under San Francisco in the BART tunnels before the city was destroyed by the sea giants, but you can't always believe what you hear in Vegas."

The customer put his face in his hands like his whole world was crumbling apart. "Are you telling me you *really* think San Francisco was destroyed by sea giants?"

Bailey's father rolled his eyes. "I suppose you hold to the earthquake theory?"

"Of course," Hanson said softly. "That's what the president said, and it's the only logical explanation. I don't believe in sea giants, or people bursting out of whales, or bogeymen, either."

Bailey's father shook his head and took the liberty of texting himself the four goblin photos from Hanson's phone. "You say you don't believe, John, and yet here you are in our store, asking us to help rid your property of a monster. We live in a newly fashioned high-tech Dark Age, my friend. The American government has become so adept at lying to the public, altering video, and disputing obvious facts with fake scientists, that it can even hide a city's destruction by two thousand-foot-tall sea giants by inventing an earthquake. But I assure you, San Francisco *was* destroyed by two sea giants seeking revenge on humans for polluting their waters. But enough politics—let's talk business. My son and I are expert monster hunters and catchers, and we would take measures to avoid as much bloodshed as possible on your property. We prefer a catch-and-release approach to monster hunting, or even better—" he said, giving Bailey a sly wink, "*catch-and-keep.*

"But if you prefer, we can offer you a suitable pet monster to protect your land and family. A pit bull isn't going to do the job here. You're going to need a real bone-cracking, blood-sucking devil-of-the-night to fight this here little villain. Although I must admit, when you fight fire with fire you can naturally expect to have twice the fire that you had before and first-degree burns are inevitable. So if you were to go that route, you'd probably end up hiring us to capture two monsters instead of one. So really, although at first it may seem to be the more expensive option, hiring us for our standard stake-out-capture-and-removal service will actually save you money in the long run."

"I just want it gone!" their frightened neighbor moaned, and Bailey grinned. He knew their customer was already hooked—no matter what price they offered.

Bailey's father took a long breath in and exhaled slowly as he pretended to consider a number. "Hmmmmmmm. Six thousand," he decided.

Bailey coughed into his hand. His father looked at him, eyebrows raised.

"Really, son? My son has done a recalculation and insists on seven."

John Hanson looked at Bailey in shock. "Seven thousand? The kid says seven thousand? I don't have that kind of money!"

Bailey shrugged. His father smiled.

"You said you live at Ahab and Blackwater?"

"Yes," their new customer said with renewed hope, putting the wisps of his hair back into place. "Can you offer a neighbor a deal?"

Bailey's father's smile turned into a sneer as he slapped his gorilla hand on the counter. "Absolutely not. If you can afford a home in *that* neighborhood, then I know you certainly can afford seven thousand dollars to remove a goblin from your property that could very well eat your children. Do you have children, friend?"

"I have a son, yes."

"If you would like to improve your son's odds of growing up to be a lawyer rather than a sandwich, I urge you to reconsider how to best spend your discretionary income."

"Okay! Okay! Seven thousand, then. Can you get rid of it tonight?"

"Yes, of course!" Bailey's father said, his smile immediately returning as he grabbed their new customer's hand with both of his and shook it vigorously. "Always happy to help out a fellow Whalefatian. Your pond, sir, will be goblin-free by morning!"

CHAPTER THREE

;)

BY THE AFTERNOON, Bailey's father was already packing for the night's camping and hunting adventure.

"Bailey, this is truly extraordinary. That guy doesn't know what he has in his backyard. I can't believe *he* is paying *us*. I'd pay *him* for the opportunity to capture a goblin. Do you know what I could trade a goblin for on the monster market?"

"But, Dad, do goblins really deserve to be put in cages? Dr. March says goblins are intelligent and that goblins love their families. He says goblins are nocturnal creatures only because they love to look at the stars—"

Dougie Buckleby picked up *In the Shadow of Monsters*, opened it to page fifty-seven, and showed Bailey the photograph of the North American tunneling goblin—boils, a grin of sharp yellow teeth, long double-jointed toes, long double-jointed fingers, ears that stretched longer than the length of its whole body. The creature in the photo sat in a hole carved out of a redwood tree. Its eyes gleamed bright green and its gums bled around its teeth. This goblin did not appear to floss regularly. The detail was extraordinary. Dr. March was a master of the telescopic lens.

"Bailey, the doctor takes a fine photo and tells a good story, but don't let him turn you soft. Monsters are creatures born of evil thoughts and deeds. This goblin would eat its own children if there were no human babies available. This *thing* would bite your ears off for its own amusement. I don't care what the famous doctor says—the man is a naive monster lover. Your mother felt the same way, always debating with me whether it was right or wrong to keep monsters in cages. You have a big heart, son, just like she did. But a big heart can leave you vulnerable to lies and dangers and an agonizing, gruesome, bloody, totally awful death."

Bailey had heard this lecture before. "I know, Dad, but Dr. March says all monsters are different. Some are evil, but some are quite friendly. Like Henry and Abigail."

"Son, Dr. March is the most famous monster hunter alive today, but he is completely wrong on this subject. *All* wild monsters are evil, vicious, and perpetually hungry. Unless you can catch, cage, and tame them like we tamed Henry and Abigail, the monsters of this world will do their very best to rip out your intestines and eat them. So watch your big heart. A goblin will eat that, too."

"I know, Dad."

His father squeezed his shoulder painfully. His grip was

so strong that it always hurt when he did that, but Bailey didn't mind. And he liked when his father compared him to his mother, but just the mention of her made his father's face fall, as if the memory of her was too heavy for him to carry.

"I need to go into the cellar and get some dynamite for tonight. Could you watch the front for me?"

Bailey's weapon of choice was the Frisbee. His father, a man with no use for subtlety, preferred dynamite.

"Of course I'm going to watch the front room," Bailey said to himself as his father went down into the cellar. "Who else is going to do it?"

The brass bell above the front door dinged again and in walked a short man in a puffy winter coat. He was bald with thick, heavy glasses. He did not have poor eyesight, nor was he cold, but he liked to increase his size with the coat and glasses to increase the fear in his customers. He was a man who loaned money to others, did favors for others, and he expected to be paid back promptly with bigger money and bigger favors. His name was Candycane Boom and he was carrying a brass birdcage covered by a thin gold drape. Something inside the cage shrieked and scratched.

"Bailey Buckleby—my favorite young adult. How are you?"

"Fine, Mr. Boom. You?"

"Excellent. Is your father around?"

"He's in the cellar getting dynamite."

"Ah."

Bailey's phone barked at him. *Roump!* Bailey had recorded his favorite monster's bark and assigned it as his ringtone for incoming texts.

Bailey! Whatchyadoin? I want to show you my social studies project!

Savannah Mistivich had been texting him a lot lately. At the beginning of the school year, she had just been a girl that he competed against in Four Square at recess. Neither Bailey nor any of the other boys could ever knock her out of the top square; she was just too fast and could really power-drive the ball. Every time Bailey stepped into the first square, she spiked the ball down in his square, and although he was fast with a Frisbee, he wasn't ever fast enough to return her serve. She laughed at him every time and Bailey had always assumed she thought he was stupid. She was probably the only person in his life who could make him feel that way.

Now he received a text from her every hour. It seemed strange, but he didn't mind. In fact, he looked forward to her texts. But he wondered why she had gone from cold to hot. *He* hadn't changed any in two months. *Unless he had.* He liked her long hair. He liked how it went so far down her back and that it flowed like the blackest ink down the back of her hoodie. Most of all, he liked that she didn't call him Monster Boy like the other kids did. In fact, she had once sent him a text that simply said: *I know they're real.* He hadn't replied, even though he so badly wanted to. His father had always told him it was safest to keep their store's backroom business a secret, although he also said monster hunting was a trade to be proud of. When Bailey was younger, his father's mixed message confused him, but now he understood the precaution was to protect them from neighbors who preferred to live in ignorance. But just because he understood his father's warning didn't mean he didn't want to rebel and tell *somebody* about their monsters. More than anybody, he wanted to tell Savannah.

He texted: *I'm watching the store.*

In one quick motion, Mr. Boom covered Bailey's phone with his stubby fingers. "Are you texting a girl?"

"No. Well. Yes."

Mr. Boom turned Bailey's phone around to read the screen, then turned it back.

"That's very good, young man, but when a customer is in front of you, you should never let your eyes off him. It's rude and actually quite dangerous."

Bailey eyed him suspiciously. "Are you saying you're dangerous, Mr. Boom?"

"Quite."

He scooted his big-framed glasses up to the top of his nose. His bald head was wet from the fog, and he was not smiling. The creature in his covered cage went *screech!* and Bailey's phone barked *roump!*

Are you ready for your social studies presentation on Monday? You know Wood is going in alphabetical order so you better be ready! :p

It was the first time a girl had texted him a *:p*.

His father came up the cellar stairs with duct tape in one hand and a canvas bag full of dynamite sticks in the other.

"Ah, hello, Candycane."

"Good afternoon, Dougie. I came to see you about possibly acquiring a friend for Bill here."

From underneath the gold birdcage drape, Bill let out another *screech!*

Dougie Buckleby set the bag of dynamite down, rubbed his hands together, and shook Mr. Boom's hand.

"I think we can do that. Yes, we have a fine selection of potential buddies for Bill. In fact, we currently have twenty-seven faeries on display."

"Twenty-seven? That's twice as many as last time. You've been on the hunt, Dougie!"

And the two men slipped past the purple curtain into the back room.

Bailey went back to reading his book, although he now had Savannah on his mind. He needed to concentrate, because he was trying to decide between one of two possible presentations.

Monday's theme was the American Revolution, and Bailey's topic was George Washington's crossing of the Delaware. He knew the story well enough to talk about how General Washington snuck across the river with his brave men, surprised the British, won the Battle of Trenton, and ultimately the war. It would be a boring and uncontroversial speech that would earn him at least a B from Mrs. Wood.

But the story he *really* wanted to tell was how George Washington won the Battle of Trenton with the help of some very special nonhuman friends. *That* presentation would be far more interesting and far more accurate. He wanted so badly to give that speech, even if it shocked his classmates and Mrs. Wood, too. She'd probably give him an F if he gave that version, but at least he'd have the satisfaction of having told the *truth* about monsters in the world for once in his life. He knew the other kids called him Monster Boy behind his back and said even worse things about his father. He knew that all of his classmates and all of their stupid parents suspected that he and his father prowled around their town at night, doing who knows what wicked things. Some knew they captured and caged dangerous monsters, but not one of them had the guts to thank them for it, even if they had hired them in the past. But as his father often said, "If Bucklebys didn't keep this town free of monsters, then who would?"

Something inside Bailey was burning. He wanted to do what he knew Dr. March would do. He wanted to give the most important social studies presentation of all time.

As if reading his mind, Savannah texted him: *What's your topic?*

How George Washington won the war.

And just how did he win the war, Bailey boy? ;)

Winky smiley face—another first. Bailey wondered if Savannah knew and believed the real history of the United States, monsters and all.

CHAPTER FOUR

THE INFAMOUS BACK ROOM

BAILEY TRIED TO ignore the shrieking coming from the back room, but it was growing louder and louder. Across from the register stood, in a perfect row for $9.95 each, driftwood replica carvings of the original Whalefatian founders who had been freed from the exploding whale thanks to Bailey's great-great-great-great-grandparents Earl and Myrtle Buckleby. Bailey moved the figurines to the counter and pretended they were his seventh-grade audience, staring him down, demanding the finest in social studies entertainment. He imagined telling them the truth and all of them jumping on him, calling him a liar and Monster Boy, then tearing him limb from limb.

The intercom crackled. *"Bailey, could you come back here and take Henry for a walk? He's too excited and he needs to poop anyway. Close up the shop for a bit."*

"Sure, Dad."

Over the intercom Bailey could hear Henry barking his anxious and excited *roump, roump, ROUMP!*

He locked the front door and turned the sign from OPEN to CLOSED. Tourists would have to buy their souvenirs elsewhere for a while—*real* business was being conducted in the back.

Bailey slid aside the purple curtain and unlocked the thick oak door with a key from his own key ring. The door opened inward to a wrought iron gate, which he unlocked with another key, which opened into their infamous back room.

Buckleby and Son's Very Strange Souvenirs occupied the first level of their three-story pink Victorian with white shingles and trim covered with seagull poop from top to bottom. The first level had once been an unpopular meat pie restaurant. Tourists used to sit and wait for their dry and tasteless meat pies in what was now the Bucklebys' front room. The former kitchen was now the infamous back room, in which long stainless steel counters with sinks at each end had become convenient easy-to-clean shelves for the Bucklebys to display their carnivorous, sugar-lusting, blood-sucking faeries.

The faeries were kept in iron lanterns and came in a wide variety of bright colors: canary yellow, fiery red, baby blue. All had stripes down the length of their chitin faery wings, which were mostly tattered from thrashing against their lantern cages in frustration. Eyes bulging red, snaggle-teeth too crooked for any orthodontist to straighten, they shrieked and thrashed and shook the bars of their lanterns. They were restless creatures, so the Bucklebys tried to keep them entertained by placing a wax candle with a long wick in each lantern. The faeries spat on the wick, which made it light since a faery's spittle contained an unusually high amount of iron sulfide. Then the faery would snuff it out. Light it with his spit. Snuff it out. Light it. Snuff it out. A faery could amuse his wicked little brain like this for hours.

His father and Candycane Boom were walking up and down the length of the counters, discussing the merits of each one. This blue-crested faery had a fierce growl. This emerald-winged mocking faery repeated every word you said, which was clever, but Mr. Boom said that in his line of work he'd rather his faeries not remember or repeat anything they might hear. This orange tiger-striped faery was missing an eye, but the empty socket made it look all the more scary. Mr. Boom brought his brass birdcage within close range of each faery to see how his own yellow-breasted faery, which he'd named Bill Collector, would react to each potential partner. As Bill was lowered within reach of each possible buddy, the two faeries would eye each other suspiciously, bare their teeth, and then reach through the bars to attempt to choke each other.

"Bill is a fierce little beast who could hold his own against whichever one you choose," Bailey's father admitted proudly. He had sold Mr. Boom his bright yellow Bill Collector just last year. "But like Siamese Fighting Fish, it's best to keep faeries in separate cages to prevent them from ripping each other apart."

24

"That will be fine," Mr. Boom said. "If one killer faery improves my debt collection rate by fifty percent, then two will surely improve my rate by one hundred percent."

Candycane Boom had earned his name with just such mad logic. He had once offered a local Whalefatian woman the choice of repaying him the eight thousand dollars she owed him or trading him her brand-new black pickup 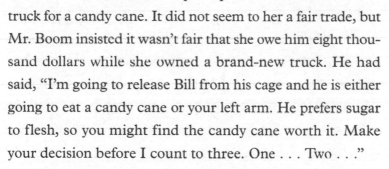 truck for a candy cane. It did not seem to her a fair trade, but Mr. Boom insisted it wasn't fair that she owe him eight thousand dollars while she owned a brand-new truck. He had said, "I'm going to release Bill from his cage and he is either going to eat a candy cane or your left arm. He prefers sugar to flesh, so you might find the candy cane worth it. Make your decision before I count to three. One . . . Two . . ."

His customer agreed, and Candycane Boom had acquired both a nickname and a brand-new truck in one terrifying moment.

"I'll take the orange one-eyed brute," he said. "I've always had a soft spot for broken, disfigured things. Jumping Jezebel is he ugly. Of course, you won't mind if I pay with *blood money*?" He pulled out a thick wad of twenties, laughing as he counted them out.

"Your money is as good as anyone else's." Dougie smiled politely. "Do you need any sugar cubes or leather gloves? Complimentary, of course."

The loan shark politely waved his hand no. "I'm already prepared. I have a pocket full of candy canes and a second birdcage. You should give these faeries more space, though, Dougie. A lantern doesn't let them spread their wings. I like my faeries fit and deadly, and that means giving them a rigorous aerobic workout every day."

"Candycane, give evil an inch and evil will take off your hand. Please be careful, my friend." Bailey's father bowed politely, removing the tiger-striped faery's cage from the counter.

"Aw, come now. Bill Collector wouldn't take off my hand."

But when he reached his finger toward Bill's chin to give him a little cootchie-coo, Bill made a swipe for his owner's finger and would have snapped it in two if Mr. Boom hadn't pulled it back in time.

"Dad, are you going to feed Abigail and everybody else?" Bailey watched Mr. Boom's maniacal smile unfold as he teased his new possession. He wondered who was more dangerous—the faery or its owner.

"Yes, Bailey. Just go let Henry stretch his legs. He's getting wild."

"Okay, because I've got to get to my social studies report."

"Don't worry, my boy. You'll have all day tomorrow. Tonight we go goblin hunting!"

Bailey knew what that meant. Staying up late, pitching camp by John Hanson's pond, catching and caging the goblin or spend all night trying, coming back to the shop, opening for business, and feeding the monsters. After all that, it would be Sunday and Bailey knew he'd be too tired to prepare at all.

Then it would be Monday, and Mrs. Wood would call them up in alphabetical order. And whether Mrs. Wood chose to call up students by first name or last, Bailey Buckleby was always alphabetically disadvantaged.

Why couldn't she go backward just once? Why did Zachary Zimmerman catch a break every single time?

If he was going to stand up and challenge the most beloved American story of all time, he wanted to make sure he had his facts straight, although his classmates would probably kill him for blasphemy anyway.

But at least he could tell himself that he had told the truth.

He shook off the worry and got Henry's leash off the hook. Henry was their seven-foot-tall Swiss troll and had been with them since Bailey was five. In fact, Bailey couldn't remember life without him. Henry lived in what used to be the unpopular meat pie restaurant's walk-in freezer. His bald blue head brushed against the top, but there was enough room in the former freezer for a chair and an aluminum washing tub. Henry loved water and spent all day in the tub, his tree-trunk-sized arms hanging over the sides, his knuckles brushing the floor, his tongue wagging happily. When he saw Bailey, he jumped out of the tub and hopped in circles and barked *ROUMP, ROUMP, ROUMP!*

Henry really was their favorite of all the monsters because he was so sweet. He was Bailey's loyal companion on walks and great for pulling him along on a skateboard and giving him big licks up the side of his face as they trotted down Oceanview Boulevard. Henry was happy to return every Frisbee that Bailey shot out to him.

Three times a day the Bucklebys served Henry a whole raw chicken in a bowl of ice water. When Henry finished his cold wet chicken lunch, he was ready to go and was accustomed to their daily routine. Bailey held up a trench coat and Henry slid his arms right into the sleeves. Then he bowed his head down, tongue wagging happily, and Bailey covered his bald blue head with a giant sunhat. Then he dropped to one knee so Bailey could add the goofy oversized sunglasses. When Bailey attached the leash to Henry's collar, he nearly fell face forward as a very excited Henry dragged him to the back exit of the shop.

"Dad, you're going to feed Abigail, right?"

His father was admiring Mr. Boom's new purchase as they both teased the little orange killer with their fingers.

"Dad? Please don't forget Abigail. Or the hoop snakes. Or the ratatoskers. Seriously, Dad, you *can't* forget to feed them again!"

Abigail the Harpy looked doubtful that her lunch would be served on time as she moved back and forth, her talons gripping and ungripping her birdcage perch. Her black-and-white-feathered wings flapped with anxiety, and her human female head cocked to the left side as she chirped madly, pleading for a sardine.

But Bailey didn't have time to insist his father pay attention as Henry practically pulled him out the back door, barking a very enthusiastic *roump, roump, ROUMP!*

CHAPTER FIVE

THE CYNOCEPHALY

WHALEFAT BEACH in September was gray and just a bit too cold, dotted with surfers in wet suits and teenagers trying to start bonfires. It was not a beach for lying out to catch sun. It was for taking spooky pictures against a backdrop of fog after a guided boat tour of the magnificent ruins of San Francisco. Bailey could barely remember how San Francisco used to look before the Golden Gate Bridge was nothing more than a humongous ball of tangled, rusted girders sitting half-submerged in the ocean, and the Transamerica Pyramid broken and abandoned, lying on its side, its tip pointing nowhere. Everyone said the video footage of the two sea giants stomping the city to rubble was fake, but Bailey knew it had been *live* and *real*.

Henry galloped ahead, using his hands as much as his feet to propel his big blue body forward. Bailey gave up and let the leash fly free. Henry wasn't going to run off. Where would he go? Henry loved Bailey and his father. Yes, Bailey's father said a troll was nothing more than a wicked and dangerous anomaly of this world, a beast mutated by evil that only wanted to eat human babies. But if his father really believed that, why did he give Henry a kiss on the forehead every night? And why did he keep raising the price on Henry's sales tag? It now read $99,999.99, an amount Bailey hoped no one would ever offer.

Bailey had secretly been wondering whether Henry was a troll at all. Dr. March had captured a wonderfully detailed photograph of a troll depicted on page 186. As the doctor's photo illustrated, trolls were indeed blue. They were taller than humans and, yes, their arms extended to their feet so their knuckles dragged on the ground just like Henry's. But the troll eyes in Dr. March's photographs were enormous and green, and their teeth were sharp and pointy. Henry's eyes were tiny and blue, and his teeth were square like white marble blocks. Hair sprouted in thickets on troll chests, shoulders, feet, and ears, but Henry didn't have a single hair on his whole smooth blue body.

But if Henry wasn't a troll, then that meant his father had either been lying to him for years or refused to accept the evidence. Whenever Bailey questioned Henry's identity out loud, his father insisted Henry was a Swiss troll and that was that. For seven years Bailey had accepted this, not because he was afraid of his father but because he loved him so much. He felt that to contradict his father was to betray him, and he never ever wanted to do that. And yet, page 186 kept nagging and nagging at him.

A couple strolled toward them along the dunes, hand in hand. Bailey sat down in the sand just below the seagrass, watching Henry run, his trench coat flapping behind him like a madman's cape. Henry looped around the couple and headed for the water. The couple ignored Henry and walked forward quickly, not making eye contact. Henry barked *roump*, *roump* in pure excitement, but his happy bark only made the couple walk faster. If they suspected Henry was a monster of some kind, they didn't want their suspicions confirmed, not when they were having such a pleasant, romantic afternoon. As they passed Bailey, the woman smiled and whispered to her companion, "He's a cute boy. Our son might look like that." Bailey ignored them with a smirk, almost annoyed that it took only a trench coat and a sunhat to hide a seven-foot-tall troll in plain sight. He doubted that humans were much smarter than monsters at all.

Seagulls flew for their lives when they saw Henry, which was wise of them, because although humans might be safe from him, Henry *would* eat a seagull given the opportunity. The birds kept a safe distance, and eventually Henry would give up the pursuit, plop his big blue butt in the wet sand, and roll around happily. When the tide would crest against him, he put his mouth down to the foam and lapped it up like Friday night dessert.

Surfers bobbed in the cold green water, waiting patiently for waves, occasionally catching one and riding it all the way to shore. Bailey shot a yellow Frisbee out in Henry's direction, just a few feet in front of his blue friend so he'd have to jump for it. Henry caught it in his mouth midair with fingers and toes pointed beautifully downward, his head held high like a proud blue retriever. He came running back on hands and feet and dropped the Frisbee in Bailey's hands. Bailey shot it out again with artistic precision, sending it just above the cresting water, and Henry went chasing after it. Allowing Henry to run and catch Frisbees made it obvious that he wasn't human, but most of the surfers bobbing in the water knew them both. If they suspected the blue creature wasn't human, they didn't care. On Whalefat Beach, if no harm was done and surfing wasn't interrupted, yelling in fright or calling the police was a complete waste of waves.

Through the afternoon fog, Bailey could see a windsurfer leaping the waves, gaining more than five feet of air with each jump. The other surfers gave him a wide berth as he tilted his rig so much that the sail was nearly parallel to the water. Bailey watched as the surfer caught a beautiful wave, pulled the rig, and flew through the air like he rode the wind. Bailey shot the Frisbee out toward Henry again as he watched the surfer fly, nearly defying physics to land just in front of Henry on the wet sand. No sooner did his board touch the beach than the surfer came running up toward the gliding Frisbee. Henry ran toward the disc, unaware of anything else around him, but the lone surfer beat him to it and snatched the Frisbee out of the air himself—*in his mouth*. It took a moment for Bailey to realize it, but while the windsurfer wore a slick black wet suit and was human from the neck down, he had the head of a dog, with a long, narrow snout and sharp-tipped ears that pointed straight up.

Henry stopped short, happy to have another player in the game. He sat on his haunches, his tree-trunk arms in front of him with his knuckles in the sand, his tongue wagging, cocking his blue head, watching the dog-headed stranger biting the Frisbee meant for him.

"Henry, here!" Bailey yelled. Henry looked at his master.

The surfer took the Frisbee out of his own mouth and held it out, offering it to Henry, trying to lure him closer.

"HENRY! HERE!" Bailey yelled again. Henry looked at him, then back at the surfing stranger wiggling the yellow Frisbee. He wagged his tongue as he tried to decide what to do. Bailey now regretted not having a longer leash so that he could reel him in.

"Here, boy! *Rowf, rowf!*" the lone surfer barked.

"Hey, man, back off,"

Bailey snapped. He was usually cool and confident, but now fear twisted inside him. He had one more Frisbee and he whipped it with a slice so that it curved in toward Henry but away from the surfer. Henry bounded toward it, snatching the Frisbee in the air like a champion and dropping it in Bailey's hand. Immediately, Bailey reattached the leash to Henry's collar and held on tight. The windsurfer walked toward them.

"That's a talented friend you have there," the dog-man said, offering the Frisbee to Bailey. "I'm sorry to interrupt your game. The dog in me can't resist a good Frisbee chase. Allow me to introduce myself—Axel Pazuzu."

Bailey shook the dog-man's hand tentatively. "Bailey Buckleby."

"Nice to meet you, Bailey Buckleby."

Axel Pazuzu sat down in the seagrass a polite distance away and vigorously shook the water from his dog head. Henry wagged his tongue, waiting for another Frisbee to fly.

"And what is your name, friend?"

"His name is Henry," Bailey said, his guard up. The dog-man seemed friendly enough, but his gold eyes looked suspiciously cunning. He scratched his dog cheek slowly as if he was calculating his next move.

"He can't speak for himself?" Pazuzu asked.

"Henry can't speak at all."

"How old is he?"

"We can't be sure. My dad bought him from another monster hunter seven years ago, but we think he's a baby."

"Ah," Pazuzu said. "He's too young to speak his language, then. It is very difficult, very old, with more compound words than even German. It took me several hundred years to learn it, but I must confess, I am easily distracted from studying."

Bailey was impressed. He had always wanted to learn a monster language, but because California public schools did not acknowledge the existence of monsters, his only choices were Spanish and French.

"You can speak troll?"

Axel Pazuzu dropped his head back and barked. Perhaps it was supposed to be a laugh, but who knew what a dog's laugh sounded like? "Yes, I know the troll language as well. But Henry is no troll."

"What?" Bailey asked, but as soon as the dog-man said it, Bailey knew his suspicions about Henry had just been confirmed.

Pazuzu waved his hand dismissively. "You said your name is Bailey Buckleby. You're the son of Dougie Buckleby, correct? And quite an expert with a Frisbee, I understand."

"Yes," Bailey said cautiously. He was starting to think this guy already knew the answers to all his own questions. Pazuzu stood up, stretched, and shook himself again. Bailey took a few steps backward, pulling Henry with him.

"So you know my dad. You know me. You think you know Henry. Who are *you*?"

"I told you, my name is Axel Pazuzu."

"Yes, but *what* are you? I haven't seen any pictures of you in Dr. March's book."

Axel smiled and looked out toward the ocean. "You're referring to *In the Shadow of Monsters*, which is a surprisingly good read, considering it was written by a human. But the word *monster* is a bit insulting to those it refers to, don't you think? I come from an ancient race of highly sophisticated beings who are not monsters at all and are, in fact, superior to humans in many ways. We call ourselves cynocephali, although humans have often called us *wind demons*, because we have outwitted humans in business and sailing so many times. We are brilliant linguists, too, primarily because we live a very long time and so have had ample time to learn the languages of all sorts of humans, animals, and what you like to call *monsters*. I myself am over three thousand years old. I suppose Dr. March hasn't written of our kind because he has never encountered us. There are very few of us left, thanks to humans, who tend to kill those they fear."

Bailey gripped his Frisbee between his index finger and thumb, just in case he needed to strike. This creature made the hair on his neck stand on end.

"Where are you from?"

"I've sailed around the world so many times, I feel like I am from everywhere and nowhere. I believe I spent my youth in Babylon, but you know, it's been so long, I can't quite remember."

Bailey had never heard anything so ridiculous. "You don't remember where you grew up?"

The cynocephaly scratched behind his ear as he laughed. "I'm three thousand years old! Can you remember even ten years ago?"

Bailey had to admit to himself that he couldn't remember that far back, and he was only twelve.

Bailey shrugged. "I guess it's true. I can't remember."

"And your blue friend is no troll—that's true, too. A cousin of mine told me I could find a very rare being for sale at the Buckleby store in Whalefat Beach, and it appears my long voyage has not been in vain. He is for sale, is he not?"

Bailey felt nervous. Here was the very question he had always dreaded.

"Technically, yes. For $99,999.99."

Axel Pazuzu's grin widened and he showed all his sharp white dog teeth.

"Then, good sir, I offer you $99,999.99. I don't have it on me in cash, but I assume you're willing to take a personal check for such a high amount? Let me just go get my checkbook—"

Bailey crossed his arms squarely and didn't even have to think about his decision. "I reserve the right to refuse you service."

Bailey did hold this right. A sign hanging on the front door of their store read in bold letters: WE HOLD THE RIGHT TO REFUSE SERVICE TO ANYONE. Another sign on the same door read: NO SHOES! NO SHIRT! NO SERVICE!

Pazuzu paused and tapped a finger thoughtfully on his chin.

"How about a million?"

Bailey's eyes grew big at the number. If he were to agree, it would be, by far, their biggest monster sale ever. They could buy another building, hire staff, and double their monster trading operation, or better yet, he and his father could go on a worldwide monster-hunting expedition to find the rarest beasts in the darkest places.

Bailey was tempted, but the thought of losing Henry was too much, so he shook his head no.

A low growl rumbled from Pazuzu's dog mouth. "Bailey Buckleby, you're being unreasonable. I've offered you *ten* times Henry's value. You are a failure of a salesman if you refuse."

Bailey was a good-enough salesman not to let a petty insult affect him during a monster negotiation. "Why do you want him so badly?"

Pazuzu ignored the question and instead looked Henry up and down. Bailey could see he was considering taking him by force. He tightened his grip on the leash with his left hand and slid his Frisbee into position in his right. The cynocephaly narrowed his eyes and tapped his dog chin again.

"Young Buckleby, although you do not realize it, your blue friend here may be the most valuable creature on the planet. And it is simply not right that you and your father keep him in a cage. You seem like an honest and upright young man—surely you see the cruelty of keeping such a beautiful beast inside a defunct freezer."

The dog-man rubbed his finger along his sharp canine tooth as he stared Bailey down. "I *will* have him, one way or another. You can either profit from the exchange or not. Worse, if you refuse my offer, harm may come to you and your father. So I ask you, why be foolish?"

"I'd say *you're* foolish to make idle threats," Bailey said sternly.

Pazuzu paused, clearly considering the odds.

"I heard you once took out a ten-foot-tall Redwood sasquatch by blinding its right eye with just one throw of a Frisbee. Is that true?"

Bailey did not realize that knowledge of his superb Frisbee skills extended outside Whalefat Beach, but he was glad to hear it.

"I'll take out your eye, too, doggie, if you lay one finger on Henry."

Axel Pazuzu growled, and Bailey growled right back. His index finger tapped anxiously on his Frisbee, adrenaline pumping through him. He almost *wanted* this dog-man to make a move. *Go ahead and try*, he thought as Henry wagged his tongue happily.

The cynocephaly nodded, deciding this was not the time. "We will meet again, young Buckleby." Then he picked up his board, ran toward the water, and in a few moments had the sail upright and was surfing out to sea as easily as he had surfed in.

CHAPTER SIX

ONE REAL MEMORY

SEVEN YEARS AGO, two thousand-foot-tall sea giants stomped on San Francisco, causing tidal waves that would leave the demolished city flooded forever. Six months later his mother disappeared and his father had never told Bailey why.

He had only one real memory of his mother, but it was a pretty good one. Perhaps most children who lose their mother at five years old would feel cheated by this, because to have only one memory of the person who loved you the most in this world is not much of a shield to ward off all the people and monsters who wouldn't care for one split second whether you suffered or struggled or died a lonely death. But Bailey's shielding memory was bright and vivid and as warm as a blanket that he could wrap himself into like a well-tucked burrito when the world was cold and dark and cruel.

In Bailey's memory, he and his mother sat under his baby-blue blanket reading his favorite book—*In the Shadow of Monsters* by Dr. Frederick March—by the warm glow of a flashlight. His father may not have shared their enthusiasm for the doctor's real-life monster stories and photographs, but that was okay. This warm moment was just for Bailey and his mom.

Dr. March's photograph took up the entire back cover. He wore a weathered cotton explorer's hat with a wide brim and glasses with thick tinted lenses that magnified a pair of wild, bulging eyes. His stories detailed wonderful legends, accompanied by sketches and photographs from the field that disproved the myth that all creatures that weren't human were wicked and cruel. Like how the peaceful and artistic labyrinth-building minotaurs fled to Africa and then to the Americas to escape all the show-off Greek heroes who had hunted them to near extinction just to impress their fathers and girlfriends, and how brilliant mathematically talented Egyptian sphinxes built the pyramids with advanced technology but suffered an entire generation of mental illness when humans put cinnamon in their drinking water. And of course the giants, the first bipeds to walk the planet, before humans, before monkeys, even before dinosaurs. Giants towered over the tallest human buildings and were made of the core elements of the earth itself.

"Mom?"

"Yes, my beautiful."

"Some monsters exist and some don't, right?"

"Yes, my sweetest of sweets."

"So which are real and which aren't?"

His mother smiled and her long auburn hair lightly brushed his face. If Bailey shut his eyes, he could still feel her hair on his cheek.

"It's a difficult question, my everything. Some people lie. Some people might invent a monster to scare you and keep you from seeking a truth they don't want you to find. On the other hand, someone might invent a story to convince you that a monster never existed, to trick you into thinking that sphinxes did not build the pyramids, or that the Grand Canyon was not created by the giant snakes of Teotihuacan, because monsters can be scary, and some humans would prefer not to believe the truth, even if it is right there in front of them. And it's easier not to believe in monsters if *no one* believes in monsters, which is totally absurd but humans find lies comforting. Understand?"

"No."

"Bailey, some monsters are real and some are not. Some will try to eat you alive, and others will become the best friends you've ever known. Monsters come in as many varieties as people, and one day, if you decide to follow Dr. March's example, you will go out into the world and see for yourself."

Bailey stared at the doctor's photo on the back cover. The eyes that looked into his were large and deep, like they had seen more of the world than anybody ever would.

"Mom, are mermaids real?"

"Yes, my perfect prince, and I pray you never meet one, because if you do, you will find her irresistibly beautiful, and you will adore her until the end of your days, which will come all too quickly as she tears your heart from your chest to eat it while you watch. Sweet dreams, my love."

Bailey's mother turned off the flashlight and the moment was over.

Huddled in a pup tent with his father in the September damp of the redwood forest, Bailey swam in the warmth of that memory. When his father turned on the rusted-but-reliable Coleman lantern, the tent glowed with a translucence that reminded him of the baby-blue blanket. Bailey loved monster hunting with his father and could not imagine a life without it. He just wished his mother were a part of it, too.

His father was laying out supplies for easy access—night-vision goggles, a rope net with interspersed lead balls to give it sufficient weight, beef jerky, orange juice, duct tape that could be used for any number of monster-hunting tasks, a bluebird night-light, a hammer, a handful of nails, seven glow sticks, and seven sticks of dynamite. His father always said it was better to have dynamite and not need it than to not have dynamite when you needed to blow the kablooey out of something.

"Dad, what do you know about the cynocephali?"

His father stopped untangling the rope net. "How do you know about the cynocephali?"

"I met one today. He had a dog head and said his name

was Axel Pazuzu. He offered to buy Henry for *one million dollars*. You might get mad, but I didn't take it. When I said no, he showed me his teeth, and I thought he was going to try to steal Henry. Then he just took off on a windsurf board."

His father suddenly grabbed him by the shoulders. "Listen, Bailey. You stay away from that *demon*. Those *things* are evil, cunning liars. What color was his head?"

Bailey shrugged. "Light brown with some white markings."

His father relaxed his grip and sighed in relief. "Okay. That was a different cynocephaly. But every last one of them are dangerous murderers. Your mother was killed by one," he said softly.

"What?" Whenever Bailey had asked about his mother's death in the past, his father had always become very sad and dark and quiet and simply said it had been a horrible, regrettable accident and wouldn't say another word about it. He had never before suggested she had been murdered.

"Dad, you've never told me any of this. I deserve to know. What happened?"

"All you need to know, son, is that the cynocephali are devilish tricksters who will lie and even murder if they can profit by doing so. I won't lose you the way I lost your mother. You stay away from this Axel Pazuzu. *Promise me*, Bailey. He's extremely dangerous, and we're certainly not selling Henry to him."

His father's big hands squeezed Bailey's shoulders

painfully hard. He knew his father loved him, but sometimes he could be so intense, he feared he would tear him in half.

"Dad, you're hurting me. Okay. I'll stay away from him."

His father let go.

"All right, son. I'm sorry. I just can't bear the thought of losing you. I love you, boy."

Bailey felt his heart swelling and his eyes filling with tears. "I know, Dad."

His father returned to untangling the rope net.

Bailey's mind was racing. To know his mother had been killed by one of these dog-headed men filled him with anger and questions. While his father whispered soft and vicious cusses at the tangled rope net, Bailey stewed over the new information, not able to quiet himself, even if it meant betraying his father's love.

"Dad?"

"Yes, son."

"Axel Pazuzu said Henry isn't a troll."

"HENRY IS A SWISS TROLL AND I DON'T WANT TO HEAR ANOTHER WIND DEMON LIE!"

His father could whisper and yell at the same time. He puffed out his chest, filling the entire tent, giving Bailey no room to breathe. Bailey didn't dare speak again, so as his father munched on beef jerky to calm himself down, he opened *In the Shadow of Monsters* to page 186. His father saw him looking at the page, and Bailey knew that simply having the book open to the doctor's entry on trolls was a silent accusation against his father, who stared at the back of Bailey's neck until he felt hot.

His father finally broke the tension, turning to put on the night goggles.

"There is one thing that all monster hunters can agree on, and that is a wicked goblin brain goes bananas for a shining light. *If* our customer's pest is indeed a goblin, these glow sticks will draw him out of hiding and right into our hands. Do you have your Frisbees ready?"

Of course Bailey did.

"The net is ready, too," his father said, leaning over and kissing him on the top of his head.

"It's just you and me, boy. You're all I have left. I'm going to protect you from all the wicked creatures in this world, *even if it kills me*. You just think about your presentation for Monday and I'll take care of baiting this little beast. You're going to do great. Hell if I know how you got any smarts with me as your father, but you're my brilliant boy with a big brain and a big heart." His father's voice suddenly got even quieter. "Your mother gave you both." Then he ruffled Bailey's hair, unzipped the tent flap, and stepped out into the night.

Bailey heard his father grumbling to himself. "*A million dollars.* Typical hot air from a typically stupid wind demon. Like a cynocephaly could hold on to so much money without losing it. Ha!"

Bailey turned off the lantern, plunging everything

into darkness. There weren't even stars in the sky. He gripped a neon-orange Frisbee in his right hand and the net with lead bearings in his left and sat cross-legged just outside the tent. John Hanson's house lights had been turned off as Bailey's father had requested. It was so dark, a goblin could be right next to Bailey, about to rip his arm off from the shoulder, leaving Bailey unable to throw another Frisbee for the rest of his days.

Twenty feet away, out in the night, crickets at the pond's edges rubbed their legs together, filling the air with their music. His father's footsteps on the damp pile of tree branches were the only clues for Bailey to tell where he was.

Then a glow stick appeared in the distance, a purple line suspended in black space. Then *tap, tap, tap* as his father nailed it to a tree. A blue stick appeared just a bit closer. *Tap, tap, tap.* A red one, a yellow one, and finally on a redwood quite close to them, a green one, *tap tap tap*. Then, at the end of the tempting, glowing arrow, the final prize to seduce any wandering goblin—the bluebird nightlight. He heard his father nailing it high up on the tree bark with a square bracket. Then the bluebird light came alive, glowing there like an angel, welcoming any lost and lonely goblin shining blue comfort. Not bright enough to be blinding, but glowing just enough to entice a goblin out of his hole. *If* one was out there.

"Bailey?"

Bailey's whispers guided his father back. "I'm here,

Dad." His father sat down next to him and put his arm around his shoulders.

"You have the net?"

"Yes, Dad."

"And your Frisbees?"

"Of course, Dad."

"Good," his father whispered. "Now we wait."

CHAPTER SEVEN

THE STARS ARE NOT YOURS

BAILEY HAD FALLEN ASLEEP. Or at least he thought he had, because no time seemed to pass before he heard the scratching of nails on bark and the grunting of something's frustration. His father was snoring. Bailey elbowed him, but he wouldn't stir. Unfortunately, his father had fallen asleep wearing the night-vision goggles, so Bailey had nothing to guide him except the soft glow of the bluebird night-light.

Was he dreaming? Because the night-light was pulsing, as if the redwood tree was one giant artery of the earth with blood flowing from ground to leaves. But the scratching grew louder, and Bailey saw the bluebird night-light was now definitely jiggling around.

Bark fell off in splinters at first, then big chunks crashed to the ground. Something inside the tree was definitely moving and earnestly attempting to get out.

"Dad!"

His father snored on, so Bailey crouched into a ready monster hunter's stance with Frisbee and weighted net ready to fly.

"Dad," Bailey whispered again. "Please wake up."

Three long double-jointed fingers burst through the bark. Then three more appeared on the other side of the night-light. The hands wrenched the bluebird free and the bark went flying. Two green eyes appeared in the dark and, by the glow of the bluebird, Bailey could see the goblin's face. Boils around its eye sockets, long ears like a mutated rabbit's stretching up, bulging eyes, and an increasing smile of pointy teeth as the goblin raised its prize up in victory.

"You beautiful blue star! I've saved you!"

Then the goblin saw Bailey.

"You can't have it. This light is mine! I'm gonna let it shine!"

"Dad. WAKE UP!" Bailey gave his father a sharper elbow to the ribs.

The goblin zeroed in on Bailey, showing his teeth. "You thief, you human boy. You're all greedy, heartless, self-centered little monsters."

"*You're* the monster!" Bailey snapped.

"The stars are not yours, human!"

The goblin crawled down the tree like a squirrel using

both hands and feet, never taking its eyes off Bailey. Then it crouched, ready to jump directly off the bark onto Bailey's face. But Bailey acted first and whipped his Frisbee precisely between its eyes. *Pft!*

"Ow!"

"The net, Bailey."

His father was awake, scrambling, trying to get himself up off the ground, but his big belly slowed him down. He grunted and pushed himself to one knee. "The net!"

Bailey threw the net just like a Frisbee, the lead weights giving it balance as it spun through the night like a perfect pizza pie. The net hovered above the stunned goblin and then brought it to the ground. Before the goblin could wrestle out from underneath the rope prison, Bailey's father belly flopped on him.

"I got you, you wicked little beast."

"Off me, fat human!"

Bailey's father had him in a choke hold, his arm around the goblin's neck. But the goblin could use its feet as deftly as its hands, so with one hand clawing at his father's arms and the other hand gripping the bluebird night-light tight, the goblin reached its left foot up and cut his fat belly with its sharp big toenail. When Bailey's father screamed and loosened his grip for just a second, the goblin twisted and turned and bit off most of his father's left little finger.

"Aargh!" The nub where his finger used to be bled profusely, but he held the goblin's neck in his elbow like a champion wrestler. "Duct tape, Bailey!"

Bailey was already peeling it off, wrapping the goblin's

ankles together. Although with its sharp toes jabbing at him like daggers, Bailey had to use a Frisbee as both a shield and a club to keep the vicious feet at bay. With the ankles bound, he went for the wrists and secured the goblin. Then his father ripped off more duct tape to bandage the nub that used to be his left pinky.

"Twenty years in the business and I've never lost a finger until today, you evil thing."

True, but Bailey's father had lost three toes in previous monster encounters. The goblin munched on Dougie Buckleby's lost pinky and swallowed.

"What are you going to do with me?" the goblin growled.

"Sell you for what the market will bear," Bailey's father said proudly. He lifted the goblin up by the duct-tape handcuffs.

"Yes, yes. Curved spine. Long ears. Large amounts of hair growth in the ears. Green eyes. This is a fine specimen of *Gobelinus cuniculus*, I would say. Good job, son. You were quite right after all."

"Dad—"

"Yes, my little friend, you will fetch a pretty penny. A rare beast."

"Dad, please look."

"For costing me a finger I would say I've earned it," his father said as Bailey removed another Frisbee, ready to fire.

"Your finger would have tasted better with honey mustard sauce." The goblin laughed.

"You're in no position to make jokes," his father said.

"Neither are you." The goblin chuckled because gleaming in the dark, just on the surface of the pond, hovered two glowing green eyes. Then another pair. Then another. In moments, at least a dozen goblin heads were breaking the pond's surface. Bailey tried to count them, but it didn't matter. He and his father were outnumbered.

"You think your friends are here to save you?" Bailey's father asked. "I came prepared."

He dropped the goblin and put a foot on him to keep him from squirming away. Then he withdrew a stick of dynamite and a lighter.

"We might leave here with more than one new pet, Bailey. It's payday."

"Dad, there are too many of them."

"Not to worry. I have plenty of dynamite."

The goblins had made it to the pond's shore. They advanced quickly, some jumping into the redwood trees from trunk to trunk, others zipping along the ground, closing in on the Bucklebys. But Bailey's father had lit the fuse.

And he threw.

CHAPTER EIGHT

YOU HAVE DETERMINED YOUR OWN FATE

A FAERY with wings as white as snow and eyes filled to their rims with blood zipped down from the night sky, grabbing the stick of dynamite in midair and snuffing out its fuse with its bony faery fingers. Bailey and his father stood stunned. The goblins looked up, just as surprised. The red-eyed faery let loose a crooked toothy smile, hovering in the air above them all, tossing its dynamite prize up and down triumphantly.

"Good job, Daisy! Very nice catch."

Axel Pazuzu stepped out from behind a redwood, wearing jeans and a nice but casual cotton sports jacket.

"YOU!" Dougie Buckleby yelled, pointing his bloody nub at the wind demon. "You conniving devil, you stay away from my son!"

"If you don't get medical attention for your injured

finger, you're going to get an infection," the dog-man said sarcastically.

"Let go of Canopus, fat human!" yelled one of the goblins.

"Let him go!" another squealed.

"Be brave, Canopus!" a tiny female goblin with the biggest green globes for eyes cried out with her fists to her mouth, which made Bailey think she cared for this captured goblin most of all.

"Mr. Pazuzu will help us," Canopus gasped from underneath his father's foot. "Mr. Pazuzu, we beg you to stop this human with your wondrous magic."

"This wind demon won't help you, you little beasts. He's more wicked than all of you and has no magic and no concern for anyone but himself."

Bailey stayed at the ready on one knee with a Frisbee cocked and ready to fly. Daisy flew in circles, salivating. Bailey knew why. Blood was sweet, and the faery smelled his father's severed finger.

"Dad—"

"I see her, son." He pushed his foot down on Canopus's back, but the goblin squirmed to get away, still holding the bluebird tight with his duct-taped hands, as if the night-light was more important than his very life.

"Oh, Daisy won't attack you," Axel Pazuzu said. "Unless I want her to."

"You and your faery stay away from me and my son."

The cynocephaly picked a flea from his neck and

flung it away. "Is this really the lesson you want to teach your son, Dougie? That every creature that is not human is evil and available for your capture, amusement, and sale?"

"I couldn't have said it better myself," Bailey's father replied sternly. "*Now step back.*"

Axel shook his dog head in disappointment. "It always comes down to physical threats with you humans. Fine, then. As an advocate for the admirable Eighteenth Goblin Order of Star Guardians, I ask you, Mr. Dougie Buckleby, to step away from gentle Canopus and return to your home. If you do not, I will have sweet Daisy here shred your belly into raw bacon and eat you alive."

"NEVER!" Bailey's father yelled, but the cynocephaly was already drawing his weapon from underneath his jacket—a plastic water pistol with a large yellow bubble chamber on the barrel. Bailey recognized the model. He played with one himself when summer days were hot enough. It was a Wylde Willy Water Blaster with rapid re-load and fire.

His father laughed. "And what do you propose to do with that?"

Axel pointed his weapon and growled softly, his canines showing. "I propose to spray you from head to toe with cherry-flavored Kool-Aid."

Bailey and his father both knew what that meant. So did Daisy, because she began to spin in circles, nearly mad from sugar lust. And the sugar content in cherry-flavored Kool-Aid was very, very high.

The goblins surrounding them—there must have been twenty by now—cheered as loudly as they could.

Axel asked again, "Please, good sir, step away from Canopus and take your son home."

Dougie stood up straight, pushing his giant foot down harder on Canopus's spine. Bailey couldn't help but worry that his father, forgetting his own strength, might crush the little goblin.

His father was red with rage. "Never!"

Axel shook his head in disappointment. "You have determined your own fate, human, as usual. *Rowf, rowf!*" And then he fired.

Everything happened at once. A stream of red Kool-Aid sprayed onto Bailey's father's chest, onto which Daisy dive-bombed with sheer delight, inhaling the rich smell of sugar water, squealing, slurping, clawing with her hands and feet and biting his belly with her sharp snaggleteeth. Dougie howled, pressing his foot down on Canopus's neck, grabbing at Daisy with one hand and his stick of dynamite with the other. Daisy let go of the stick. She didn't care about it; she cared about one thing only—*sugar*. She bit and bit and bit, and Dougie's wounds opened, his blood mixing with the Kool-Aid.

Bailey drew a neon-green Frisbee and shot it with perfect precision so that it sliced at the last moment into the cynocephaly's neck. Choking, unable to breathe, the wind demon dropped his blaster and grasped for his throat, giving Bailey a moment to stand up and flick his last Frisbee straight into his right eye.

"*Bow wow wow . . . owwww!*" he howled, grabbing his injured eye, turning, and running into the night.

Then the goblins leapt.

They grabbed Dougie's arms and legs, piling on him while Daisy shredded his Kool-Aid- and blood-soaked shirt with her sharp, crooked teeth. The tiny goblin dove for his right foot, trying desperately and unsuccessfully to pry it off Canopus's neck.

"Canopus! My darling!"

"Can't breathe . . . can't breathe."

Canopus struggled and squirmed under the big man's weight. The goblins piling on them only made it worse.

"Can't breathe . . . Help, Capella . . . help."

Big-eyed Capella held Canopus's hands and pulled and pulled, but Dougie's foot was firmly planted on her beloved's neck.

Bailey tried to drag the goblins off his father, but there were too many in the pile. He feared his father would suffocate and bleed to death if left much longer. But Bailey had a monster hunter's instincts. He crawled into their tent, grabbed the lantern, and then crawled back out. He stood up and turned the light to HIGH so it blazed brightly, lighting up John Hanson's entire backyard.

He could see the goblins in vivid detail now—the boils on their green skin, the hair sprouting from their long pointy ears, the double-jointed fingers and toes that held tightly on to his father. All at once, their glowing green eyes turned toward the lantern, mesmerized. In unison, they sighed: "Oooooooh!"

59

"What a beautiful star!"

"Star of the night!"

"Shining so bright!"

"By our souls, we will save your light!"

The goblins squirmed off Dougie and came running toward Bailey, but before they pounced on him, he threw the lantern as far as he could into the redwoods. The goblins immediately changed direction and ran toward it. "Star light! So bright! How your light awakens the night!" They piled on the lantern, all grabbing for it and abandoning Canopus. Only Capella remained, tugging on his arm.

Daisy continued to bite and bite, while Bailey's father cussed at the vicious little faery. But then Bailey grabbed the weighted net and scooped Daisy off him, tied a quick knot, and had her captured.

"Thank you, my boy," he said, lifting Capella up by her ankles. She wiggled desperately to squirm free.

"No, Capella, NO!" Canopus yelled.

But Bailey's father had them both, holding them upside down in the air, grinning with pride.

"Well, I'd call this a successful night," he said. "Not one goblin but two. And we got the demon's pet as well," he said, poking his bloody finger stump at Daisy. "Come on, Bailey. Let's go home and lock up these little wretches."

Bailey looked at his father, soaked in blood and Kool-Aid, his shirt shredded, his wounds bleeding as he held a goblin by the ankle in each hand, his sweaty shag of rusty hair in his eyes. For a moment, Bailey saw his future.

In twenty years, would he be soaked in blood, missing a finger, holding captured, frightened monsters upside down by their ankles? He wondered—would his mother approve? But she was dead and his father was alive, so he told himself it was childish to guess.

CHAPTER NINE

THE WONDERFUL LIGHTED PAINTBRUSH THAT GOD USES EVERY NIGHT

BAILEY COULD BARELY keep his eyes open. It was dawn. Abigail wanted her sardine breakfast, Henry wanted his raw chicken in ice water, and the twenty-six faeries wanted sugar, as always. The hoop snakes needed live mice, and the live mice needed kibble. The ratatoskers needed fresh vegetables from the garden. Abigail chirped like mad, the faeries squealed, and Henry barked *roump, roump, ROUMP!* Daisy wailed loudest of all, banging against the walls of her new iron lantern prison. She was the only white-winged faery on display, and Bailey's father had hung her lantern high above the others from a ceiling hook and priced her for her rarity at $9,999.99. Daisy swung her lantern back and forth, screeching and spitting iron sulfate on the floor below to create tiny flashes of fire. But the two goblins—Canopus and Capella—each sat quietly in separate wire cages designed originally for large dogs, staring at the long fluorescent lights in the ceiling.

Bailey, though tired, got busy making their breakfasts. The sooner the monsters were fed, the sooner he could sleep, and the sooner he slept, the sooner he could wake up to work on his presentation for tomorrow. Savannah had texted him *Are you ready? ;)* He had texted back *Sorta.*

His father, having suffered significant blood loss from his finger, had microwaved a pepperoni pizza, eaten it, and fallen asleep upstairs.

After Bailey fed Abigail and Henry and all the faeries, he came to Capella's cage. She seemed to be more responsive than Canopus, who only stared at the fluorescent ceiling lights with his mouth gaping open, salivating, occasionally reaching his double-jointed fingers up in longing for the lights. Capella crouched in a corner of her dog cage, hooding herself in the fleece blanket Bailey's father had given her, as if trying to resist the temptation of the shining fluorescence.

"Would it be better if I turned the lights off?" Bailey asked. "Do they hurt your eyes?"

"No, you mustn't do that," Capella gasped. "Stars were meant to shine. Don't darken the stars on our account."

"What do you mean? They're just electric lights."

Bailey demonstrated his point by walking to the light switch and flipping it several times to make the lights flicker. Canopus screamed in horror.

"Please don't torture the stars," Capella pleaded. "It's

bad enough you keep us in cages, but to starve the stars is the worst of all possible crimes."

He and his father had never captured a monster that spoke English in complete sentences before. He felt guilty for caging such intelligent creatures.

"We put you in cages because our customer paid us seven thousand dollars to keep you off his property and stop you from stealing his lights."

Capella grabbed the bars of her cage with her long fingers. "No one owns the stars! We were simply trying to do a good deed. The best deed! To save lives. *To save the stars.*"

Bailey crouched down and sat cross-legged in front of her cage. "You keep saying that, but don't you realize these lights aren't stars? They're electric bulbs. They're made in a factory somewhere by people—*by human beings.*"

Capella turned away from Bailey. "You humans take credit for everything. *You* didn't make the stars. The stars of the night used to shine so bright. There used to be millions. Now when we look up, we only see a hundred or so. Soon there will be no stars left. You humans have knocked them all down. Someone has to take responsibility, don't they? We are the Eighteenth Goblin Order of Star Guardians, and we mean to put the stars back in the sky before you kill them all. And before you kill all of us, too."

Bailey scratched his head. "I think you're a bit confused."

"I think you're a typical human," Capella said. "Greedy. You say we steal, but you stole the stars first.

And now you're even stealing us. Our tunnels once stretched throughout the whole world, connecting all our tribes. Now we are separated by human construction. Your subways destroyed our homes and your sewers flooded our cities."

Canopus stared upward, reaching his long fingers through the cage bars.

"You're going to burn your eyes out if you keep staring. Can I get you two anything to eat before I go to sleep?" Bailey asked.

"I'm not hungry," Capella said. "Canopus? Are you hungry? The human boy wants to feed us."

But Canopus didn't say a word. He still clung tightly to the bluebird night-light, which glowed from the power of a single AA battery, although his eyes remained fixed on the even brighter, blazing, eye-watering ceiling lights.

Bailey was too tired to insist, and his eyelids itched. He locked the wrought iron gate, locked the thick oak door, slid the purple curtain behind him, and dragged himself up the stairs to his bedroom.

He climbed into bed and turned to page fifty-seven of *In the Shadow of Monsters*, where *Gobelinus cuniculus* stared back at him with sharp teeth and large green eyes. Bailey read the lush words of Dr. Frederick March:

Having established camp several hundred feet below the peak of Mt. Lyell in the Sierras, I found myself slightly dizzy from the crisp thin air at thirteen thousand feet and the anticipation of my first sighting of Gobelinus cuniculus. *The sun had set, re-painting the big sky behind the mountain peaks in yellows, oranges, and purples. I remained half-buried in snow and dirt, trying to remain as hidden as possible, with my trusty Nikon D700 camera at the ready. Scratched-out holes in fallen redwood trees pointed me toward the subject I sought. I knew from my studies that these holes were the surface exits of tunnels that extended through the tree cores, past the roots, deep into the earth. Sure enough, as the sky grew darker, goblin heads began to appear. I remained perfectly still while one by one their heads popped out of the tree holes. They nodded to one another in greeting, their ears long and pointy and at attention. Darker and darker the sky softened and more and more goblin heads appeared. Their nightly theater was about to open. The stars began to appear, at first only a few scattered pinpoints of light above the silhouettes of mountains. I dared not even take a single photo yet for the simple fear that my camera click might attract their sensitive ears and scare them away.*

I waited. More and more stars appeared, filling the night sky with light, and just as our children might enjoy the grandest fireworks display on Independence Day, they ooohed and aaahed at the show. Their excitement and laughter and amazement grew, and soon they were clapping loudly as the Milky Way burst into view and the sun disappeared entirely. Only a thin crescent of the moon remained to provide any other source of light. Humankind's artificial light is absent in the Sierras, so the stars' majesty could not be muted. The goblins' clapping was excellent auditory cover for me. I began clicking my camera, capturing their rows of sharp teeth. I have never seen such an impressive display of sharp serrated teeth except on the great white shark. Their long ears wiggled in the cold night, their green eyes glowing and reflecting their love, their gods, their greatest happiness. I watched several goblins hold each other tight in warm gratitude for the display. Several smaller infant goblins huddled closer to their mothers, asking their parents about the wonder they were witnessing. Was this their own dialect of English I was hearing? I could not believe my ears! But I dared not approach any closer.

I stayed behind, although I desperately wanted to join in their reverie. I nearly shed tears for love of the stars myself, as if I was seeing them for the very first time, never before having contemplated the wonderful lighted paintbrush that God uses every night to illuminate our infinite sky. No wonder these goblins never failed to make this appointment. I stayed with them unseen until dawn, taking photographs. I did not want the accursed sun to rise, because as the coming sun's light changed the sky from black to blue, the goblins dropped back into their holes one by one, disappearing from my sight. As dawn took the place of the night, the mountain peaks of the California Sierras— though majestic in their own right—suddenly seemed to me so lonely and far too bright.

Bailey stared at the doctor's photos of the goblin eyes peering up at the Milky Way for as long as he could, but his own eyes were very heavy. He pretended that he himself was Dr. March, grown-up, wearing muddy hiking boots, a vest with a hundred pockets, a camera around his neck, huddled in between logs in the mountains, a discoverer of goblin hideouts and beautiful views of the stars. He wondered where the great international monster hunter was now. In the hills of Afghanistan? The jungles of the Congo? Somewhere beneath the sea? Bailey wondered if he himself would ever leave Whalefat Beach to seek out the most exotic monsters yet unknown to humans, and maybe even meet Dr. March along the way.

Bailey reached his hand down beneath his bed to find a shoebox hidden there. He opened it to remove a photograph his mother had taken seven years ago. It was a picture of Henry in diapers, blue and smiling with his long tongue hanging out. His mother really did take a good photo.

Then he turned to page 186 to Dr. March's entry on trolls. The troll in his photograph crouched underneath a rustic bridge, its blue body camouflaged in mud, partially hidden by trees. One arm of the troll reached up the length of a tree, its long, muddy fingers blending with the overhanging branches, so that if an unsuspecting human were to attempt to cross the bridge, the troll could quickly grab the trespasser, crush his bones, and eat him whole. Long, straggly hair hung from the troll's head, ears, and armpits. Bailey placed his mother's photo of Henry side by side with the photo of the troll. Yes, they were both blue with long arms all right, but unless Henry was about to undergo an incredibly transformative and unfortunate bout of puberty, Bailey just couldn't see how Henry could grow up to become this horribly hairy, sharp-toothed ugly beast.

Thinking about the mystery made him even more tired, and before he could shut the book, he was asleep.

CHAPTER TEN

BABOON BUTTS

BAILEY WOKE UP at four a.m. He had slept through the afternoon, evening, and a good portion of the night. Dread for the school day crept down his spine and into his stomach. Today was social studies presentation day.

He checked his phone. Savannah Mistivich had been texting him. *Are you ready? 9:11 p.m.* Then again: *Hey boy are you ready? 9:29 p.m.* Then one more time: *Well good night you little punk! You better be writing some good stuff! ;) 9:58 p.m.*

He liked that she had sent him three texts. He saved them and reread them several times.

All the lights in the house were on as he went downstairs. He heard his father's classic rock music blaring from the back of the shop, where bright light was shining from beneath the purple curtain.

The faeries snored, their tattered wings over their little heads to shield themselves from the fluorescent lights. Abigail tucked her human head down into her wings, too. The hoop snakes and ratatoskers hid in their nests of wooden shavings. Even blue Henry lay snoring in a corner of his walk-in freezer, his head covered by his feet, which twitched as he undoubtedly dreamed of chasing seagulls and lapping up sea foam.

But Bailey's father was wide awake, sitting on a stool in front of Canopus's cage with his sketch pad on his knee. Bailey had always liked his father's sketches because they showed such detail and captured real monster emotion as vividly—if not more so—as Dr. March's or his mother's photographs. It seemed ironic to Bailey that his father's illustrations portrayed such feeling, since he always said all monsters were evil and should be locked up. And even though Canopus had chomped off one of his father's fingers, his sketching ability had not diminished. His portrait of the goblin was coming along nicely and looked quite lifelike.

Many of his father's drawings had been published in the monthly magazine *Peculiar*— a publication that catered to the small niche of monster fans who knew full well that monsters really did exist. The magazine

featured wonderfully detailed articles about monsters from around the world, debates concerning their locations and histories, and a very useful classified section for monster sellers and buyers. Dr. March and Bailey's father were frequent contributors, although they had never met each other in person.

Dougie hoped his goblin sketch would catch the eye of the editor of *Peculiar* and might even earn him the cover.

"I'm going to make you a star," he whispered to Canopus, but the goblin didn't seem to hear. He still clung to the bluebird night-light and stared at the ceiling lights. His eyes had swollen to slits from the bright light and lack of sleep. Bailey feared he might go blind.

"Dad, how long have you been up?"

"Hours, son. I was too excited to wait until morning. I hope I didn't wake you."

"I wish you would have. I slept yesterday away and I have my presentation today. I've run out of time to prepare."

His father squeezed his shoulder and shook him. "I'm sure you'll do fine. You can think on your feet, just like you did on the hunt when you threw the lantern to distract the goblins. You saved my life, son. Your mother would have been so proud. Just look at him, Bailey—*in our possession*—the infamous *Gobelinus cuniculus*."

Bailey looked at Canopus's swollen eyes and pitied him and his crazy ideas.

"Dad, you know why these goblins are obsessed with

lights, right? They think the stars fell out of the sky and it's their job to put them back."

His father continued sketching. "How do you know that?"

"Because the female one told me so."

His father swept the hair out of his eyes. "Don't let a goblin fool you, son. She'll say whatever is necessary to trick you into opening the cage. Think of them as dumb moths, drawn to lights out of instinct. And remember, if given the chance, she'll eat your face."

"Maybe we should turn the lights off so this one doesn't go blind."

Bailey's father looked up from his sketch pad as if to see his subject for the first time.

"Agreed. This little guy is going to burn his eyes out and we don't want a defective specimen. He doesn't know what's best for him. You're a good boy, Bailey. Go upstairs, write your presentation, and I'll feed everybody this morning. Even you, *Gobelinus cuniculus*, will get a square meal from the Bucklebys, although you did bite my finger off. I was fond of that finger, you know. What's your presentation on, son?"

Bailey hesitated. "How George Washington and his trained yeti won the Revolutionary War."

His father sucked in a big breath. "I don't know if you want to tell that version."

"Dad, I know what you're going to say—"

His father put his hand up to stop him. "It's not just

that I want to protect the family business from scrutiny, Bailey—I'm trying to protect *you*. I'm proud that you know how the yeti helped Americans win the war. The yeti—as bloodthirsty as they are—deserve our eternal gratitude for the part they played in our country's fight for independence. But you know how mean kids can be. They'll turn on you rather than hear the truth."

That's just what Bailey was afraid of. And yet, he almost wanted a fight.

Seven o'clock arrived. Bailey put on his hoodie, grabbed his backpack and skateboard, and pushed off down wind-blown Oceanview Boulevard toward John Muir Middle School.

He heard the sound of a skateboard coming up on him and immediately knew who it was. His heart beat just a little faster.

"Hello there, Bailey boy."

"Hey, Savannah." Bailey stood up as tall as he could on his board.

Savannah was still taller than him. In fact, a lot of the seventh-grade girls were taller than Bailey, but knowing he could fight off a horde of goblins, a wind demon, and a bloodthirsty faery with just a Frisbee and his wits gave him the courage to look directly up and into Savannah's eyes, which shone a beautiful brown and seemed to reflect the whole world. He wanted to look in those eyes forever. Except he couldn't help but be distracted by the worn leather-bound trombone case tied around her chest and shoulders with nylon rope. Bailey knew she didn't play trombone in the school band, but he was impressed she was able to ride her board like that without falling off.

"What's in the case?" he asked.

"It's no trombone. I'll tell you that much, Bailey boy."

Then Savannah did lose her balance. She pushed forward when she should have braked, and her board shot forward, she fell backward, and she rolled onto the sun-bleached asphalt.

Bailey stopped. "Are you okay?"

She stood up. Blood soaked the left knee of her blue jeans, but she didn't cry out at all. She was more concerned with the trombone case, which she unlatched and peeked into. Satisfied that what was inside had not been disturbed, she quickly latched it shut before Bailey could see.

"This is my A+ project."

"What is it?"

"Like I said, it's no trombone." She grinned wickedly. "Where's your project?"

Bailey tapped his temple. "All up here."

"So you're still not ready."

Bailey sighed. "No."

And Mrs. Wood wasn't giving out any free passes. She sat behind her large metal desk like a gargoyle ready to take a swipe at the face of any student who dared suggest that maybe they could postpone the presentations and just watch a movie instead? Her hairdo was outdated and her glasses were too small for her beady eyes, reminding Bailey of one of the mole people featured on page 142 of *In the Shadow of Monsters*. Even her skin was pale and pasty like a mole person, and she grumbled quietly like a broken toaster with bread stuck in the bottom that could catch fire at any moment.

As Bailey and Savannah slipped into their seats, Ella Robertson, who wore ribbons in her hair and had a tiny face, asked her what a trombone had to do with the Revolutionary War. Savannah told her to mind her own goofy Ella Robertson business.

"Aaron Aackerman!" Mrs. Wood bellowed. Nothing.

"AARON AACKERMAN!" No response. Bailey groaned to himself. How could Aaron be absent today of all days?

"Bailey Buckleby!" Mrs. Wood barked.

Bailey willed himself invisible like the giant chameleon salamanders of the South Pacific featured on page twelve.

Bailey pulled *In the Shadow of Monsters* out of his backpack and walked past Savannah's desk to the front of the class. As he passed her, she smiled and whispered, "*Good luck, boy,*" and he immediately stood up straighter.

Everyone stared at him, the boys smirking and the girls already bored. Only Savannah smiled at him like he was a rock star. He took a deep breath and rolled his shoulders back.

I can do this.

He closed his eyes and let the words come.

"The Abominable Snowman saved America!"

A long horrible pause, then the class laughed in unison.

Savannah hissed, "Shut up, you dingleberries."

Bailey opened his eyes. Mrs. Wood and Savannah and

the whole class were still there—waiting. He took a deep breath and continued:

"George Washington was the greatest general and yeti tamer of our country, and yet no history book in our school recognizes the fact that without the yeti of New Jersey, the Revolutionary War would have been lost. The yeti—commonly known as Abominable Snowmen—were originally natives of the Himalayan Mountains. Yeti are ten feet tall on average, covered in white fur, and have claws as hard as stone. Male yeti have tusks instead of canine teeth, while females just have regular yeti teeth. Many yeti, minotaurs, and other monsters were transported through Africa and then to the American colonies on slave ships to be sold as exotic pets to plantation owners. However, some yeti escaped and traveled to colder climates like New England. Yeti like snow and often live in caves and suck on icicles like Popsicles. George Washington and fifty of his bravest men climbed to the peak of High Point, New Jersey, to find yeti and tame them with frozen cherries and rum and Virginian tobacco cigars, because it turns out that yeti like smoking as much as humans do. Then George Washington and his soldiers saddled them and used their incredible yeti strength to fight the British—"

"This is a bunch of bull, Monster Boy!" Derek Whiffle threw a wadded-up piece of paper at Bailey. Derek had black eyes, no hair, was constantly sweating, and when he showed his teeth, too many of them came to sharp points. He looked a bit monstrous himself.

"Mr. Whiffle! You DO NOT raise your voice or use

foul language in my classroom! Nor do you throw things at your classmates while they are presenting."

Mrs. Wood's face had turned red, and her hands had become claws. If this had been a classroom in cold New England during the time of George Washington and the yeti, laws of corporal punishment would have allowed Mrs. Wood to smack Derek upside his head, which she would have surely done. Instead, she slammed her right claw down into Jenny Lester's papier mâché replica of the Liberty Bell and put a much larger historically inaccurate crack in it. Jenny burst into tears immediately, because she had spent all week on that stupid Liberty Bell without any help from her mother. She stood up, crying, and ran straight for the girls' bathroom without a hall pass.

Savannah stood up to make her voice heard.

"You shut up, Derek! Let Bailey finish!"

"MISS MISTIVICH!"

"Your boyfriend is lying," Derek said. "He's telling lies that are un-American! There are no such thing as yeti or any other monsters! My father said—"

"No one cares what you and your dumb father think. You both look like baboon butts!" Savannah yelled.

"MISS MISTIVICH! MR. WHIFFLE!"

Bailey was stunned momentarily. Did Derek just say *boyfriend*?

"I have pictures," Bailey said quietly. He lifted up his beloved well-read, worn-cornered *In the Shadow of Monsters*, opened it to page 288, and held it up high to show the class the detailed pencil sketching of General Washington and his fifty brave men offering rum-and-cherry Popsicles and Virginian tobacco cigars to the yeti of High Point, New Jersey. In the sketch, one of the yeti sat on an ice throne with a cigar and lifted a Popsicle up to toast his new buddy, General George Washington.

Derek Whiffle stood up. Most of the class was laughing by now.

"Liar! Traitor! You're telling lies about George Washington, and that's treason against America!"

Derek had gotten himself very worked up and was about to cry with passion.

"But I have proof," Bailey insisted.

"Miss Mistivich, you SIT DOWN! Mr. Whiffle! DOWN!"

Savannah stared directly at Derek Whiffle, and the rest of the class looked horrified. No one was looking at Bailey anymore.

"You and your father are the liars," Savannah said sternly. "There *are* monsters in the world. *You* can pretend like there aren't, but everyone in Whalefat Beach knows *your* father hired the Bucklebys to rescue *your* mother from a Redwood sasquatch who had kidnapped her two years ago. But I bet he told you that story wasn't true, either."

Derek started whimpering and stuttering. "It's NOT true. That's another Monster Boy lie!"

"You should be thanking Bailey, not yelling at him,"

Savannah continued. "I bet your daddy told you San Francisco wasn't destroyed by sea giants, either."

"Damn right! San Francisco was destroyed by an earthquake!" Derek's voice squeaked in fury.

"LANGUAGE!" Mrs. Wood screamed at the top of her lungs.

Then Ella Robertson stood up and spoke very evenly. "No, Savannah is actually right. San Francisco *was* destroyed by sea giants, because the Bucklebys practice black magic. *They* worship the devil, and *they* raised the sea giants up from hell, and thanks to them, millions of people had to run for their lives. We should kick the Bucklebys out of the country and make them take all their evil demons with them."

"No, Ella," Bailey said quietly, with his beloved book still above his head. "There are monsters, but there is no such thing as black magic. At least, there is no scientific reason to think so."

But no one could hear Bailey over the impending riot. All his classmates started giving their opinions at once. Some said yes, they had seen the sea giants marching toward the city with their very own eyes. The nonbelievers called them liars who should shut up, and then the believers called the nonbelievers babies who should grow up. Ella and Savannah both remained standing, staring at each other with pure venom.

Then little Billy Dolby stood up. "San Francisco was destroyed by an earthquake caused by the oil companies, and that made the sewers explode. The oil companies did it!" Billy's voice was the loudest of all, which surprised everybody, including Mrs. Wood, because tiny Billy Dolby hadn't said a word all year.

"No," Bailey said matter-of-factly. "You can still see the sea giants if you just take a boat trip. The Farallon Islands are right in the ocean where they used to be, but they're not actually islands. They're the tops of the giants' heads. They settled back there after they retreated."

"Bull turds, Monster Boy!"

"MR. WHIFFLE!"

"Listen to Bailey for just one second, you buttheads!" Savannah yelled.

Ella covered her ears, closed her eyes as tightly as she could, and screamed, "The Bucklebys are evil! The Bucklebys are evil! THE BUCKLEBYS ARE EVIL!"

"EVERYBODY QUIET DOWN!" Mrs. Wood stomped to the front of the classroom and put her hands on Bailey's shoulders, pushing him forward just hard enough to let him know his presentation had ended. He walked past Savannah to his seat, and everyone quieted down as reality set in—Mrs. Wood was quite capable of punching her fist through more papier mâché projects, and no one wanted to risk that. Everyone sat and tried to stop laughing from the awkwardness of it all. Only Savannah and Ella remained standing in their tense stare-down.

"Miss Mistivich. Miss Robertson. *Please.* If you would each like to take a five-minute break and walk around the playground to cool your heads, you may do so."

The class let go a short burst of laughter. The girls didn't accept the offer, but they did finally sit down.

Mrs. Wood ended social studies early, which made everybody happy because nobody else had to give a presentation that day. Everybody was happy, that is, except Bailey and Savannah. Mrs. Wood gave Bailey a B– for causing such a disruption and not finishing his speech, even though she had been the one to end his presentation prematurely. She did compliment him for sparking an interesting class discussion, which every good social studies presentation should do. Savannah was upset because she hadn't gotten to reveal what was in her trombone case.

At the end of the day, Bailey and Savannah slowly skateboarded across the cracked and weed-infected basketball court toward Oceanview Boulevard.

"I'm sure you'll get to show off your secret project tomorrow."

"Actually, I might need to use it right now," she said.

Bailey saw where she was looking. The four high school bullies had skipped their afternoon classes to come to John Muir Middle School and wait for Bailey, no doubt wanting revenge. Bailey dropped to one knee to open his backpack and ready four Frisbees, one for each of the thugs' foreheads.

But Savannah moved faster than him and already had her trombone case open.

CHAPTER ELEVEN

THE BULLHEAD BRIGADE

"**YOU'RE GONNA LISTEN** to us this time, little seventh grader."

Fuzzy carried a baseball bat. Burper wielded a formidable tree branch. Chinless and Caveman had nothing but their fists, but they clearly believed those would be enough. As the four thugs marched toward them, Bailey felt the adrenaline of fear fill his body, even though he had confronted five times as many goblins last Saturday night. Frisbees might not be enough ammunition this time. But then the sophomores stopped dead in their tracks, staring at Savannah. Bailey turned to look, too.

Her right hand gripped the hilt of a sword, a weapon more than two feet long that looked quite old and spotted with rust but still very, very sharp. The blade was blackened steel, the hilt polished wood with a silver tracing that curved and ended in the head of a bull. It was a soldier's sword and yet Savannah Mistivich—seventh grader with semi-decent skateboarding skills and mostly C's on her report card—handled it with ease. She swung it in front of her like she was fighting off one hundred redcoats.

"Get back, you British hooligans."

None of the sophomores were British, so they looked at one another in confusion.

"Back! Back!" Savannah advanced, and the boys stepped back. Bailey dropped to one knee with a black Frisbee cocked and ready to fly, surprised by Savannah's bravery.

"What do you think you're gonna do with that?" Fuzzy seemed to have forgotten that he was carrying a baseball bat. Other middle schoolers were approaching the chain-link fence, attracted to the smell of a possible fight. The sophomores didn't want an audience. Even if they thought they would win, high schoolers beating up seventh graders was not a good look.

Savannah was breathing heavy. "Do you . . . want to sing . . . like Michael . . . Jackson?"

"What are you talking about, you weirdo?"

"One by one . . . with this sword . . . I'm going . . . to make . . . each one of you . . . castrato."

The boys had mostly D's on their report cards, but still, they knew that vocabulary word and it wasn't good.

Savannah screamed and charged, swinging her blade like the bravest militiawoman of the thirteen colonies.

Bailey didn't even need to throw his Frisbee before all four turned and ran. He had to chase Savannah for four blocks and grab her arm to stop her or she would have run after them all the way to whichever 7-Eleven they called home base.

"Okay, okay. They're gone," Bailey said, and they both fell to the ground, laughing. Flat on her back with adrenaline still pumping through her, Savannah waved the sword up in the air.

"Isn't it great, Bailey? It's a Mistivich family heirloom. Check out how perfect it is. I like how it feels in my hand. It's a 1765 hanger sword that American officers used during the Revolutionary War. Some swords were stolen off British officers by American soldiers, but this sword was made by a blacksmith in Boston. See the bull head? That signifies the Bullhead Brigade that my great-great-great-great-grandfather was a member of. They were the bravest of the bravest soldiers. The British were so scared of them, and they had such a reputation for being so fierce, that they were nicknamed the Bullhead Brigade. Some even said that half of them weren't even human and had the heads of bulls. And I'm directly descended from one of them!"

Bailey couldn't believe it. "You know the history of the minotaurs in America! You were going to give a speech about monsters in history, too!"

"Yeah," she sighed. "I was pretty excited to see the looks on their faces. Who knows *what* Ella Robertson would have called *me*! Are you that surprised, Bailey boy? I told you I knew monsters were real. Monsters are in my family!" She swung the blade back and forth slowly, watching it shine in the after-school light coming down through the eucalyptus trees.

"It's probably good you didn't get a chance to give your presentation, Savannah. I don't think swords are allowed on school grounds. Even fake ones. And that is a *real* sword."

"It's a family heirloom, which makes it totally different," she said.

"Why do you keep it in a trombone case?"

"So no adults at school would know I was carrying a sword."

The wind off the beach cooled their sweat. Bailey reached over to touch Savannah's wrist, but she jumped up, waving her sword, before he could even consider more.

"Let's go. I think I just saved your butt and you owe me." She put her great-great-great-great-grandfather's blade back in the trombone case. "I want to see it."

"See what?"

She raised her eyebrows. "You know exactly what I mean. I want to see what every kid in this town wants to see whether they will admit it or not—the famous back room of Buckleby and Son's Very Strange Souvenirs."

Bailey smiled like he had a secret, which of course he did, and it was exciting to finally be able to share it with somebody. He was glad that somebody would be Savannah. He dropped his skateboard to the sun-bleached asphalt and pushed himself down Oceanview Boulevard. Savannah Mistivich grinned and, without another word, put her board down and followed.

The afternoon was blue and the Pacific fog had burned off. Vacationing families that had just seen the magnificent ruins of San Francisco had heavy hearts and some nice photos and now wanted to stroll down the sidewalks of Whalefat Beach and maybe find a tasty barbecued whale blubber sandwich. Kids wore foam whale hats and parents wore beach-ready shirts they had bought that morning. Bailey saw that there were customers in the front room of their shop as he and Savannah skated up. The faeries' shrieking, Abigail's chirping, and Henry's bass-drum barking could be heard from the front door. The mothers and fathers from out of town looked simultaneously curious and concerned, but Savannah giggled like Halloween had just been rescheduled for this very afternoon. Dougie Buckleby, sweating and overwhelmed, could not work the cash register.

"Oh, thank goodness, Bailey. I need your help, son. This register refuses to cooperate with me. We'll be right with you, good folks. You will love that hot sauce, ma'am, I guarantee it's delicious on pizza. We'll ring you up here in a moment—BAILEY!"

"Hold on, Dad."

While Bailey jumped over the counter and took over for his bewildered father, Savannah dropped her board by the door and floated down the aisles like she was in a dream. Without hesitation, she drifted past the confused tourists, past the T-shirts and flip-flops and fake whale blubber, to the source of the sounds that she knew instinctively did not emanate from cats or dogs or an extra-large parrot.

Bailey rang up the twelve-pack of gift-sized Whalefat Beach Blazing Bonfire BBQ Sauce bottles while simultaneously watching Savannah's hand reach for the purple curtain. The family of four left the shop as quickly as possible to escape the terrifying noises that inclined them to drive straight back to Idaho without taking a single rest stop. Bailey watched Savannah pull back the curtain and reach for the doorknob of the thick oak door that lay behind it.

Of course, the door was locked.

Bailey's father gave a friendly nod to the next customer in line as Bailey rang up her hermit crab purchase.

"Your girlfriend is the curious sort."

"She's not my girlfriend, Dad," Bailey said, rolling his eyes.

His father waited for the line of customers to finish before he said any more.

"Bailey, I've always known that eventually you would want to share the world we know with a girl. But it's important you understand that girls are going to come and go, and for a handsome, intelligent boy like you, they're going to fall in love with you quite easily."

"Dad, you can stop now—she's just a friend from my class."

His father grabbed Bailey's head with his meaty

four-fingered hand and shook it like it belonged to a teddy bear who was immune to concussions.

"A monster hunter leads a dangerous life. He has to protect his heart, so take one piece of advice from your old man—women can be more dangerous than monsters, so don't fall in love until you're at least thirty."

"DAD!"

His father stood up straight, chuckling at his son's embarrassment. He gave Bailey one raised eyebrow and then marched proudly to the thick oak door.

"Let me unlock that for you, young lady. Bailey will be happy to show you around. Watch your fingers."

His father held open the door and unlocked the wrought iron gate on the other side. Savannah stood up on her toes and Bailey scooted by both of them so that he would enter first and be the one to show Savannah what lay beyond. His father squeezed his shoulder as he passed. Bailey tried to play it cool, but he was excited to see just how she would react when she saw them all.

And when she did see them, all she could do was put her hands together and whisper with pure joy—"*Yes.*"

CHAPTER TWELVE

CHIRP CHIRPETY-CHIRP

"DOES SHE FLY?"

"She flies," Bailey said.

"Does she speak English?" Savannah gasped.

"No. She just chirps like crazy. All day long. See the white feathers on her belly and her wings with black tips? My dad thinks that she and the sea osprey have a common ancestor. It's his theory anyway. I don't know what Dr. Frederick March would think."

"Who's Dr. Frederick March?" Savannah asked.

"My role model. He's the author of the book on monsters that I read from today. And kinda who I want to be when I grow up." Although Bailey felt that familiar guilt for contradicting his father as soon as he said it.

"You really are a beautiful lady, Miss Abigail. I'm very happy to meet you. Can I feed her?"

"Sure. She goes nuts for sardines." Bailey reached for a tin from the cupboard, stopping a moment to listen to the intercom. If he heard a faint crackle of static, it meant that his father was listening with a cloth over the speaker, a method of eavesdropping that his father believed, incorrectly, was clever enough to fool his son. But Bailey heard nothing, which meant the back room was entirely his kingdom to show her.

He rolled back the tin key and she removed a slimy sardine without hesitation.

"You like sardines, beautiful lady? Look how she cocks her head! I think she understands me."

"I don't see how she could," Bailey said. "She's half bird, which means she's half as dumb as a bird, which means she's not smart enough to understand English."

"What an awful thing to say!" Savannah punched Bailey hard in the shoulder. "Bailey Buckleby, don't you call her dumb! She has a bird body but a *human* head, which means she must have the best features of both. She has a human brain in that beautiful lady head, don't you, beautiful Miss Abigail?"

In fact, Savannah was entirely correct. Abigail did have a bird body but a human brain and did have sufficient faculty

for the interpretation of language. What neither Bailey nor Savannah nor even Abigail knew was that a harpy has a syrinx in her throat rather than vocal cords. So although the rest of her anatomy from the neck up, including her brain, was human, her syrinx was entirely bird, allowing her to chirp, sing two notes at the same time, and even breathe *in* while singing *out*. She was a talented creature. She did not have the capability to speak English or any other human language, but having spent the past two years with the Bucklebys, she was starting to understand English quite well and was excited to now have Savannah's attention. Madly, she sang Savannah all of her concerns: *Where am I? Is this mirror in my cage the portal to a parallel universe where another one of me remains captured? Will I ever be set free so I can return to Greenland? And could I have more sardines right now, please?*

Of course, these concerns formulated in her human brain but were expressed through her bird syrinx, so all Bailey and Savannah heard was *chirp, chirp, chirp, chirp, chirp chirpety-chirp?*

"She seems to have a lot to say," Savannah said, handing her another sardine.

"I wish we could let her out to spread her wings, fly around, and get some exercise, but she would probably fly off and never come back."

"Would that be so bad?" Savannah asked. "I bet she misses her family."

Abigail responded in the positive. *Chirp, chirp, chirp, chirp CH-CH-CHIRP!*

"My dad would be furious. He traded a ten-foot-tall one-eyed Redwood sasquatch for her."

"But what if she has children?"

"You mean chicks?"

"Or boys."

"No, I mean—"

She left Bailey mid-thought to walk down the aisle toward the faeries, each of which tried to impress her. One gnashed its crooked teeth at her, one spit at a candlewick, sparking it into flame, another yelled *"Hee-yaw!"* and kicked a ball of its poop out of its lantern prison right at her nose. She dodged the poop ball instinctively and effectively.

"These little guys are nasty," she said.

"Very nasty," Bailey agreed. "Some monsters can be tamed, but not these guys. They'd rip your face off the first chance they got."

Bailey showed her the hoop snakes and how you could pick one up and turn its end to its mouth so that it would clamp on to its own tail with its jaws and then stretch itself into a perfect circle. He set a clamped hoop snake down on the floor and it whizzed to the other end of the room. Savannah laughed as the snake did a 180 and came careening back toward them like a wild tire. They lifted their left feet to let it pass, then their right as it returned, then their left again until it tired itself out and Bailey put it back in its terrarium to chill out.

"Who are these little cuties?" Savannah asked. She had found the ratatoskers, which had rat bodies and ivory tusks that curved up, stretching their upper lips into sneers.

"They're originally from Norway and can travel for hundreds of miles. If you give a ratatosker a letter, it won't drop it for any reason."

"How does he carry it?"

"You puncture the letter on his tusk and then he knows he has something important to deliver."

"How does the little guy know where to go?"

"Well, Dr. March says ratatoskers have the best sense of smell of all monsters. So if you have any piece of clothing worn by the person you're trying to reach, a ratatosker can pick up the scent. Then you let him loose and off he goes to deliver your letter. Ratatoskers have internal GPS systems, kind of like how birds know to fly south, and they'll swim across an ocean or cross a whole bunch of mountains to get to their destination. Nothing will stop them from delivering your message."

"I like them." Savannah smiled, rubbing each of their soft heads. "They're like fuzzy miniature mail carriers."

When they came to Henry, he was already jumping up and down, ready to meet a new friend, his fists on the floor to hold him steady, his tongue wagging and wagging.

"Look at this big blue boy!"

With too hard of a squeeze, Henry could crush Savannah into jelly, but she showed no fear as Bailey unlocked the door to the former freezer and Henry bounded out, licking their faces.

"He smells the ocean," Bailey explained. "It gets him wound up for a run. Let's go."

Roump, roump, roump!

Savannah couldn't believe her luck. "We're going to the beach? With him? I've pretended to have a monster to play with my whole life. I never dreamed I'd get to for real!"

Bailey smiled proudly as he took down the leash, the trench coat, the giant sunhat, and the oversized goofy sunglasses. Savannah practically fell on the ground laughing as Bailey held up the coat so Henry could slip his tree-trunk arms into the sleeves, missing them twice in his excitement.

"This blue guy is something else."

"Henry's our favorite for sure."

"I like him, too," Savannah said with a grin.

Bailey pressed the red button on the intercom.

"Dad, we're going to walk Henry."

"Okay, son," his father said from just behind the wrought iron gate, where he had been spying on them the whole time. This annoyed Bailey a bit, but Savannah didn't seem to care. She kept patting Henry on the shoulder.

"You wanna go for a walk, boy? Go to the beach? You're a happy blue boy, aren't you?!"

Roump roump roump!

Henry wasted no time showing off his strength, pulling both Bailey and Savannah by the leash as he lunged forward on all fours. He practically dragged them down Oceanview Boulevard, through the seagrass and gravel and onto the damp sand. His tongue-wagging determination nearly made Savannah trip and fall, so Bailey scolded Henry, yelling, "Henry, calm down, you maniac!" He couldn't wait to show Savannah how much Henry loved the beach and the ocean no matter how cold the water was.

Until he saw who was there.

Axel Pazuzu, in his black wet suit, stood where the water met the sand. The cynocephaly faced twelve goblins bobbing in the water, each one of them wearing snorkeling masks.

CHAPTER THIRTEEN

THE UNIVERSAL CURRENCY

STANDING TALL and with excellent posture, Axel raised his dog head proudly. With his black wet suit on and a patch to cover his Frisbee-damaged eye, he looked like a formidable pirate as he barked orders at the goblins.

"Duck down, you scrubs! You have to get used to the cold water and the waves. Dive! Dive! Dive!"

Seven of the goblins dropped down below the surface of the water. The other five didn't hear or were just too scared to obey. "Dive!" Axel Pazuzu barked again, and Bailey could see that the goblins were also wearing wet suits as well as human-child-sized oxygen tanks on their backs. The wind demon was teaching the goblins to scuba dive.

Henry splashed into the surf in pure happiness, lapping up the sea foam.

"Whoa! Who are you? I love your ears!" Savannah said, running up to the cynocephaly as if there could be no possible threat. Axel bowed deeply to her.

"Keep back, Savannah. This is a dangerous, lying wind demon," Bailey said, but Savannah wasn't scared of anyone and she had never seen a dog-headed man before.

"Axel Pazuzu, miss. And who might you be?"

"Savannah Mistivich."

"An honor to meet you, Miss Mistivich. And young Mr. Buckleby—so good to see you again," he said, bowing to Bailey as well. "Though you gave me such a shiner, I fear I may never see out of this eye again." He lifted the eye patch so that both Bailey and Savannah could see the bulging red tomato that was once, but no longer, a functioning dog eye.

"*You* did that to him?" Savannah gasped.

"Yes. This demon tried to kill my father." Bailey unclipped a Frisbee from his belt.

"I did indeed. I would ask your forgiveness, except that retaliating against your father was simply part of the job for which I have been hired. The Eighteenth Goblin Order of Star Guardians has asked me to protect them and aid them in their quest to put the stars back in the sky. Your father hunted down and captured two of the Order's members. I am being paid to protect and aid, so I came to the rescue. Unfortunately, I have failed so far, and so these shrewd goblins are withholding my pay. But I assure them and you, Bailey Buckleby, that I will rescue both Canopus and Capella, as well as my beloved Daisy, and provide my fine employers with the means to put the stars they love so dearly back into the heavens. You should really let Capella and Canopus go. They are, after all, just hardworking, innocent goblins."

Bailey's blood was boiling, but he managed to keep his temper in check. This manipulative cynocephaly had badly hurt his father and he did not forgive so easily.

"So you're their bodyguard?" Savannah asked.

"Well, Miss Mistivich, I am their bodyguard but also their adviser. I like to think I've learned a thing or two in my long time on this planet. My knowledge is useful to some but comes at a price."

"Don't try to hurt my father again," Bailey said, anger shaking him. "Or I'll take out your other eye."

The goblins stood completely out of the water now, and they started to move forward, but Axel raised his hand to halt them. It did not appear to Bailey that he was a hired bodyguard. It seemed more that he was completely in charge. Henry, oblivious, chased a seagull in circles.

"Of course, it is natural for a human like yourself to have such violent instincts, Bailey. You must defend your family, as I must defend mine. Or at least the family that has hired me."

"You can't buy your way into a family," Savannah said, her voice rising.

"Can't you, dear? We are each members of many families. We call our blood relatives family because they give us a roof and meals. Our employers because they give us money. Our neighbors because we share land and mutually hate other neighbors. We fight for those who give to us; we war against those who take from us. I am a very old cynocephaly, so I have seen many families kill one another over the years. But never have I seen a family take so much as the human family. You humans have taken so much of this world for yourselves, you've killed off many of its species and nearly all of mine. I've always been a fan of the underdog, and today, I assure you that the Eighteenth Goblin Order of Star Guardians is the underdog in this fight. *Rowf!*"

"You only like the goblins because they pay you," Bailey said.

"Yes, of course. Well, not yet. They've agreed to pay me in gold after delivery of service. Everyone loves gold, especially humans! So it really is the universal currency. Don't be so judgmental, Bailey. You receive pay to be in your family as well."

"My father loves me. My father is my *real* family."

"And your father pays you with kindness, food, and shelter. If he did not, you would be taken away by child protection services. But since he does pay you, you repay him by trying to be a well-behaved son and cleaning up faery poop."

"Nobody loved you as a child, did they, Mr. Doghead?" Savannah asked.

Axel scratched his doggy chin. "You know, it's been so long, I can't quite remember."

After a long, horrible pause, Bailey asked, "Did you know the cynocephaly that killed my mother?"

The wind demon's pointed ears stood straight up in the air. "Is that what your father told you? We cynocephali are the smartest salesdogs to sail the seven seas, but we are *not* murderers. But I'm not surprised your father would make such an accusation."

Bailey's blood was hot, and he felt rage flowing through him. "You attack my father and then call him a liar?"

The wind demon looked at the back of his hand and licked it calmly. "I do indeed call him a liar if the label fits. Seven years ago, my cousin Willard sold a baby to your father for a very handsome price. Your mother, however, thought the sale was unethical, so after six months had passed, she took the baby from your enraged father and fled. Now, once the sale was made and Willard had his gold, he did not care what became of the baby, but he happened to see your mother sailing away from Whalefat Beach as fast as she could with your father hot on her tail. Willard, who is not usually the compassionate sort, took pity on her and called upon a whale to protect her. But your father, in his anger, threw a stick of dynamite at Willard's boat, and my cousin barely escaped with his life. In the confusion, your poor mother was swallowed by the whale and, I assume, digested. And your father, a man with no ethics at all, took the baby home and told you that he was a troll and not what he really was—a baby sea giant, kidnapped from his parents."

The wind demon turned to study Henry, who was

wagging his tongue obliviously. "I believe our dear blue Henry here is the baby in question."

Bailey was so angry he could barely speak. "You're lying, just like my father warned me. I don't believe you . . ."

"Of course you don't, Bailey," he said softly. "Your instincts tell you to believe your father, not me. I only hope he doesn't make any more selfish decisions that will cause him to lose *you*. We may be able to prevent such a horrible eventuality at this very moment because I would like to make you another offer. How about two million dollars for your large friend?"

Savannah put her hands on her head. "Two million dollars? Are you serious?"

The wind demon stood up straight and adjusted his eye patch with a snarl. "*Quite* serious."

No amount of money could impress Bailey now. He was sure that this demon was a liar and probably didn't even have that much in his possession anyway.

"No," Bailey said, a Frisbee spinning slowly on his thumb. "I don't know why you want Henry so badly, but I'm sure it's for a reason I wouldn't like."

The cynocephaly looked out to the ocean where the Farallon Islands rose in the distance. "Then I will have to proceed to making the purchase indirectly."

"Indirectly?"

"You won't sell Henry to me, but he must be mine so that I may help the Eighteenth Goblin Order of Star

Guardians put the stars back in the sky. The baby sea giant is a key element to our plans."

Bailey couldn't believe what he was hearing. "The goblins think that man-made lights are fallen stars. You and I both know that's ridiculous."

Axel bark-laughed. "Of course it's ridiculous! Stars are giant orbs of burning hydrogen and helium. But I am to be paid in gold to assist them, so who am I to question their science? Anyway, I've convinced them that your blue friend Henry is essential to their task. Your father won't conduct business with a cynocephaly ever again, so I must pay a human to make the transaction for me. In fact," he said, looking at his waterproof watch, "my hired human is most likely outlining the terms of the purchase to your father at this very moment. I suggest you bring Henry back to your shop so that the sale can be promptly concluded."

Then he leaned in close to Savannah's face. "Unless we act sensibly, avoid all possible bloodshed, and I just take him right now."

Savannah put her nose to his. *I'd like to see you try.* Then she bopped him in his eye patch with her fist.

The cynocephaly howled in pain. "How dare you! You'll pay for that someday, little girl!"

Axel turned back to the goblins, who had been creeping toward Bailey and Savannah. He kicked sand at them. "Get back in the ocean, you disobedient whelps! You need to be certified dive masters by Thursday!"

CHAPTER FOURTEEN

PUNKS

"**WE SHOULD ASK** him what he's gonna do with those little green guys," Savannah said.

Bailey shook his head. "They're the Eighteenth Goblin Order of Star Guardians. We need to get home and tell my dad right away. He warned me cynocephali were dangerous liars, and now I think he's right. I don't know what he means by 'indirect purchase,' but it sounds like a trick."

They ran faster, with Henry gallomping excitedly behind them, hoping for a Frisbee to catch. He couldn't know Bailey felt an urgent need to inform his father that Henry's sweet life of chicken in ice water and walks on the beach was in dire jeopardy. But just as they reached the store, the four delinquent sophomores slid out from behind a eucalyptus tree like panthers on the prowl.

"Well, well, well. It's little Bailey Buckleby and his female bodyguard. But you forgot your sword this time, didn't you, girl?" Fuzzy hissed, and he was right. She had left her trombone case in the back room of the shop.

"We have something better than a sword," Savannah yelled. "Fear the wrath of Big Blue!"

Savannah pulled off Henry's trench coat, a move that wasn't as graceful as she might have liked, and pointed to the boys. "Get 'em, Henry!"

Henry sat down on his back haunches and panted.

"Henry's not the aggressive type," Bailey said calmly, unclipping a yellow Frisbee from his belt.

"We know your stupid pet isn't dangerous. In fact, we know just what he likes," Fuzzy whined like a tenth grader without a girlfriend. Then Bailey saw what Burper was carrying with both hands—a bucket of ice water in which bobbed several whole raw chickens.

Henry had a belly full of seawater, which he liked very much, but his breakfast had long since been digested. His eyes bulged, and the sight of the chicken pulled him like gravity. Bailey tugged on Henry's leash, but that slowed him down no more than the ocean breeze. Luckily, the back door of the shop opened, and his father came out with his left hand behind his back and a lit stick of dynamite in his right.

"The fuse is burning, boys. Off with ya."

"You're bluffing," Caveman sneered, but all four of them took one step back.

Bailey's father looked them each up and down. His size was intimidating, let alone the stick of dynamite in his hand.

"How could I be bluffing? There's no stopping a gunpowder fuse. This dynamite is going to explode somewhere. Now, boys, consider your dilemma. I can only throw this dynamite so far. I'm not going to let it explode behind me—that would be foolish. So this stick is going to explode in front of me, somewhere within a forty-foot radius because that's as far as I can throw. Within this forty-foot radius, in which you are standing presently, there's going to be a big explosion. Now, do yourselves a favor and consider a simple question—what happens to the human body when it is within forty feet of a dynamite blast?"

Now even Savannah was scared. She stepped behind Bailey's father into the back room.

Each of the four sophomores shuffled their feet, not wanting to be the first to calculate the distance required to escape certain death. Bailey's father waved the stick in his right hand and barked, "GO!" which was enough to make them sprint as fast as their legs could carry them, even into oncoming traffic on Oceanview Boulevard, which luckily was only the snow-cone guy on his tricycle. The snow-cone guy toppled over, his box of flavored ice spilled into the street, and he yelled, "PUNKS!"

Bailey's father pulled his left hand from behind his back. He was holding a green-bellied Amazonian faery by the neck and squeezed it so the faery coughed and grabbed the fuse with its miniature fist, snuffing the fuse right out.

"Dumb little deviants," Bailey's father spat. "Get inside, Bailey. We need to fortify."

"What do you mean? You just scared them off."

"They're just thugs on the payroll, son."

"Dad, seriously. Not one of those goons even passed pre-algebra."

His father shut the door behind them, locked it, and then swung the iron latch bar down to block it.

"Call your girlfriend's parents. She needs to get home as quickly as possible." He started lifting boxes from beneath the stainless steel counters to free the space below.

"Also, I need you to get on your hands and knees and find the valve that raises the wall."

"Dad, what are you talking about?"

"Just get down and look for it. It's blue with a label that says NOT WATER."

"Is this all about Axel Pazuzu? Is that who you're afraid of?"

His father paused and sat on the damp cement floor. He was sweating already.

"I'm not afraid of anyone, Bailey. I'm a Whalefatian and, what's more, I'm a Buckleby, and Bucklebys are always prepared for their enemies. Those boys must be working for him, and he must be working for Pazuzu, because only a wind demon would care this much about Henry."

"Who's *him*? Who's working for Pazuzu?"

His father wiped the sweat away from his forehead. "Candycane Boom, son. He left his calling card."

CHAPTER FIFTEEN

THIS WRONG MUST BE RIGHTED

BAILEY FOUND THE candy cane sitting by itself on the store counter. The bubble gum, the mints, the Whalefat Beach playing cards, and the miniature whales made of soapstone had all been shoved off the counter and onto the floor in one violent sweep. The front door was shut, locked, and barred with an iron rod just like the back door. The sign in the window had been flipped to CLOSED. Bailey returned to the back room, locking the thick oak door and wrought iron gate behind him.

His father was on his hands and knees, pushing away boxes and electrical cords, looking for the mysterious valve. Savannah looked out between the slats of the blinds while Henry sat on his haunches near her and licked her face.

His father handed him a piece of stationery that was

decorated with fine calligraphy that read *From the Desk of Mr. Candycane Boom*. Mr. Boom's handwriting was elegant and in cursive, which Bailey could read even though John Muir Middle School had elected last year not to teach cursive writing in their classrooms anymore.

To the honorable Mr. Dougie Buckkby,

As your friend and customer, I hope you will understand that if I am forced to make any physical threat against you, it is only because I anticipate that you will fail to comply with the following:

I do hereby request that you deliver dear Henry to me this afternoon in exchange for one candy cane. It has come to my attention that you keep Henry from his parents and you imprison him in a walk-in freezer. My friend, even I find this act incredibly inhumane. This wrong must be righted. Also, as a hired consultant of a mutual associate, it is only my duty to inform you that the physical threat I hereby make will be bloody and painful. You have stolen a son and broken two hearts. Please do not force me to break yours. I will be waiting outside with my staff.

Most sincerely,
Candycane Boom

Bailey had always known Mr. Boom used the threat of violence to make a living. He should have guessed that he and his father weren't immune to the danger he posed.

As if reading his thoughts, his father said, "Candycane has always been just a loan shark and a thug. When a shark is hungry, it turns on you."

Bailey was starting to feel a horrible, sickening, nauseating feeling—doubt in his father. "Is it true? Are we keeping Henry from his parents?"

Dougie looked rattled as he searched for the wall valve, as if the very question made him angry.

"It's a wind demon lie. This is what they do. They feed us lies and turn us against each other."

Bailey unleashed Henry as he thought about what he was about to say very carefully.

"Dad, I think you and I both know that Henry isn't a troll. Henry has blue eyes, square teeth, and not a single hair on his body. And I don't think Axel Pazuzu would be so determined to get Henry if he *was* just a troll. So tell me—what is he?" Bailey suspected he already knew the right answer, but to make this horrible feeling go away, he needed his father to say it.

As if curious himself, Henry jumped up and down on his haunches and barked *roump!*

His father sighed. "Bailey, you are your mother's son in so many ways. But I will tell you what I told her—*the truth*—and that is that Henry is a long-armed, blue-skinned, seven-foot-tall baby Swiss troll who we have tamed quite well and is now a member of our little family. Trust me, Bailey, when I say that all I've ever wanted was to give Henry the same two things I give you—safety and love. Aha! I found the wall valve!"

Bailey shook his head, determined not to let his father avoid the question. "Dad—"

"There are angry people outside," Savannah whispered, peering through the blinds.

"Young lady, it is time for you to go home. I'm sure your parents are worried about you."

Savannah's voice became sad and distant. "My parents aren't home. They're getting remarried."

Bailey's father looked up in shock. "Remarried? To each other?"

"They divorced last year, but then they went to couples counseling. Now they're getting married again in Cabo San Lucas. They told me it would be good for me to learn how to live alone."

"But you're just a kid!"

"I'm fully capable of taking care of myself!" Savannah exclaimed. "I'm twelve years old, you know, and what's more, I'm a descendant of the Bullhead Brigade. I'm certainly strong enough to live alone for a week!" But even she knew it wasn't right, and she was glad to be with the Bucklebys, even if they were quickly being surrounded by enemies.

"Where have all the responsible parents gone?" Bailey's father groaned. "It seems, orphan girl, that perhaps you should stay here after all."

"I think so," Savannah agreed, more from excitement

than fear. "The mob out there is growing. I'm going to get my sword out. I've been waiting for just the right time to use it!"

Bailey looked for himself. On the opposite side of Oceanview Boulevard, Cheri's Chocolates had guests, but not the usual assortment of tourists. The four bullies hovered there like rabid raccoons. Fuzzy took a few practice swings against one of the supporting porch beams with his baseball bat. Burper slouched on the bench, sharpening his tree branch into a deadly point. Caveman counted off push-ups while Chinless threatened to sit on Caveman's head—bare butt. In the middle of the porch stood Candycane Boom in his puffy winter coat, big glasses, and smooth, hard head. He held a bag of gourmet chocolates, which he ate by the fistful. From inside, frightened storeowner Cheri looked out the window at her unwanted customers. Bailey doubted Candycane had paid for those chocolates.

When Boom saw Bailey and Savannah looking out the window, he pointed at them, and the four sophomores followed the direction of his finger. With a mouthful of chocolates, he yelled, "GO!"

The four sophomores got in position to charge. Fuzzy twirled his baseball bat above his head, Burper waved his sharpened tree branch, and Caveman and Chinless made fists and put their heads down like angry bulls.

Bailey couldn't believe what he was seeing. "I think those idiots plan to break through this window."

"I'd like to see them try," his father cried, cranking the

wall valve with both hands. The valve had tightened from rust and years without use and took all his father's gorilla strength to budge it even a millimeter. But when it finally began to give, he started turning it faster, and soon they all heard something beneath the floor squeak as it scraped against metal. Then the sound of rushing water let loose beneath them. *Clank* . . . . . . *clank* . . . . . . *clank* . . . *clank, clank, clank.* The water pushed open metal doors underneath the floorboards and a rushing sound filled the walls, travelling vertically, as the water moved upward.

"Seawater." His father smiled. "Piped in directly from the ocean. It's going up the pipes and turning the water wheels on the roof that pull the pulleys."

"What pulleys?" But Bailey already knew the answer. He used to play up on the roof when he was younger, though his father never knew, and sometimes he'd walk as close as he'd dared to the edge of the roof with his eyes closed to test his own bravery and instincts. He had found the eight large metal rusted wheels connected by copper cable—two wheels at each corner—and had guessed they had been put there by someone who had owned their shop long ago. Now he heard the big rusted wheels creaking into use for the first time in years. The pulleys pulled and the copper cables began to move.

"Raise the blinds, orphan girl!"

Savannah did so and cried, "Ah!" She raised her 1765 Boston-crafted hanger sword and gripped the hilt with both hands as the boys sprinted toward the window at full speed with weapons and fists raised.

Bailey reached for a Frisbee on the counter, but it wasn't needed. His father continued to crank the valve as steel planks connected by iron chains unfolded neatly and quickly, raised by the copper cables to form a wall around the entire building. *Clank, clank, clank!* The water wheels turned and the pulleys pulled and Dougie Buckleby giggled like a kid. Then they heard four loud thuds as the boys piled into one another and hit the steel plank wall. Chinless muttered a disappointed "Aw, man." In just seconds, Buckleby and Son's Very Strange Souvenirs had become an impenetrable fortress.

CHAPTER SIXTEEN

THE MACHETES

"**GET UP, YOU RUNTS!** Hit 'em again! Flying Florence, what am I paying you for?"

Candycane Boom paced in front of Cheri's Chocolates as he yelled at the four sophomores through his megaphone. But the four boys looked at one another dumbfounded. Even if they had paid attention in school, they wouldn't know how to penetrate a steel fortress.

Bailey's father opened the window and yelled through the thin crack between the protective steel planks. "You're dealing with the Bucklebys now, Boom. We are the real Whalefatians, prepared for all forms of wickedness and devilry!"

He turned to Bailey and Savannah in excitement, his eyes wild, like he was enjoying this.

"Okay, kids. Buckleby's is fortified on all four sides, but not the roof. So we will climb up there and make our stand."

"On the roof? For how long, Dad?"

"As long as it takes," his father said firmly. "If Earl and Myrtle Buckleby could live in a whale for over a year, then we can certainly make camp on a roof for at least as long."

Bailey didn't like the sound of that. He did hope to pass the seventh grade someday.

"We will need supplies. Get the tubs of peanut-butter-honey mix, Frisbees, and sardines for Abigail. Most of all, get Henry and as many raw chickens as you can carry. He must not leave our side! I'll get dynamite and Abigail, too."

His father pulled a purple velvet hood over Abigail's cage so she wouldn't be scared. In her confusion, she whistled, *Chirp?* Henry, loving all the activity, jumped up and down on his hands and feet, shook his head, and barked *roump, roump, ROUMP!*

They climbed the three flights of stairs, past the bed-rooms on the first floor, past the second-floor library stuffed to the ceiling with all his father's leather-bound monster tomes, rolls of monster trail maps, and piles of past issues of *Peculiar*, and up to the third floor, where a hatch could be opened to access the roof. Bailey's father pulled down the narrow unfolding stairs that allowed them to climb up and through the hatch. The stairs were almost too narrow for him and that was doubly true for Henry.

As Savannah pushed Henry through the hatch, she said, "You've got a big blue butt, Big Blue!"

Three stories below them, Mr. Boom and the four sophomores looked up at them from the porch of Cheri's Chocolates. Cheri and her chocolate-making assistants stood watching the scene unfold. Bailey's father gave them a friendly wave. Cheri had hired Dougie many times to clear sugar-crazed faeries out of her kitchen. She was one of the many Whalefatians who needed the Bucklebys' monster-hunting service, whether she wanted to admit it or not.

"We may want to bring up some chairs," Dougie said, peering over the edge of the roof. "We could be here a good long while."

Bailey wondered how long he was supposed to ignore the resentment quickly growing inside him, as if he was being dragged into a dirty secret that changed everything he ever thought was true. If Henry had been kidnapped from his parents as Mr. Boom's note had said, his father could very well be responsible. That made Bailey an accomplice—he was a partner in Buckleby and Son's after all. He had never known life without Henry in it, but now felt guilt for taking a child from his parents, even though he was just now learning about the crime.

He couldn't stand on this roof another minute with his father without confronting him.

"I've got to hear you tell me the truth, Dad. Henry's not a troll, is he? He's the son of the two sea giants that destroyed San Francisco seven years ago. I know it's true, Dad, but I need to hear you say it."

His father didn't look at him. His face was turning red, like he might cry. Or kill somebody.

Bailey wasn't going to let up now. "You've known all this time, but you kept him anyway."

"Son—" his father started, but neither one of them could say anything more.

Savannah broke the silence, shouting at the little mob below. "You can't have Henry!"

Boom raised a megaphone to his lips. "YOU SHOULD STAY OUT OF THIS AND GO HOME, LITTLE GIRL."

"I'm no little girl! I'm a twelve-year-old proud Bullhead!" she yelled loudly, defiantly, waving her sword. Bailey ducked, just to be sure he kept his head. "Why don't you just go away and leave the Bucklebys alone!"

Bailey's father chuckled. "You've got a feisty girlfriend here, son. I like her style."

Bailey shook his head. "I know what you're doing, Dad, but I won't let you ignore me. Ignoring me is just as bad as lying to me. I'm more than just your son. I'm your business partner. If you're keeping a baby sea giant from his parents, and they destroyed a city to find him, and if you're responsible for Mom's death, you *have* to tell me. I'm not a kid anymore—I deserve to know."

It took everything Bailey had to stand still. His gigantic father looked at him as if he was searching for any words that would get him out of this predicament.

"I'll tell you when the time is right, Bailey."

Bailey would not let go. "I think that time is *now*, Dad. In fact, you should have told me a long time ago."

His father got down on one knee. "You're right, son. You *do* deserve to know. But first, I'm going to light this dynamite."

His father already had a stick in one hand and a lighter in the other. The fuse was four feet long, and with a flick of his thumb, the lighter lit, and a spark started to run up the length of the tightly twisted, oiled string.

"Son, let me tell you something. We are Whalefatians. We are descended from a people that have always known that humans would be extinct if they did not take a harsh view of monsters. This peaceful little town of surfers and candy vendors and barbecued whale blubber sandwich-makers wouldn't have been possible at all unless brave heroes took out their machetes and cleared a path through a jungle of evil. We are directly descended from those heroes. Bucklebys have always been willing to wield the machetes, knowing full well no one would thank us for doing so. We are the vanguard."

The spark traveled up the oiled string and Savannah bit her lip. Bailey tried to concentrate on what his father was saying.

"Our people *did* escape a giant whale. The stories are true, despite what all the nonbelievers say. Your great-great-great-great-grandparents Earl and Myrtle Buckleby were swallowed by one of the biggest giants to ever swim the seas, then they blew it to hell, swam to shore, built this town, and raised a family in the face of the bloodiest of horrors. California used to be plagued with all kinds of wickedness back when it was completely wild. The first Whalefatians fought off sasquatches trying to steal their women, goblins that devoured their children, and sugar-mad faeries as rampant as flies. And you and I both know how bloody carnivorous faeries can be. *Evil is real.* The government and our neighbors want to pretend like monsters don't exist and never have existed, but they do, and even if they don't want to admit it, our neighbors need us."

The spark only had a few more inches of oiled string to travel.

"Dad, answer me. Is Henry the baby the two sea giants have been looking for?"

His father looked him in the eye and held his shoulders firm.

"No, son. Henry is a Swiss troll. Your mother believed otherwise, and now you're tempted to believe otherwise, because evil wind demons lied to you both. You can't believe everything you hear. You know I don't talk about your mother's disappearance because it's the saddest moment of my life, but you're right—you do deserve to know.

"Henry had been with us for six months and your mother, just like you, saw a few traits that weren't quite troll-like. We argued about this for days until one stormy morning the same cynocephaly that sold Henry to me lied to her and said she was right, that Henry had been kidnapped from his parents and Henry's parents had destroyed

San Francisco trying to find him. The cynocephaly said he would return Henry to his parents, but of course this was another lie—he wanted to keep him for himself to sell again. Your mother decided to try to return him herself, although I pleaded with her not to. She borrowed a boat but that evil wind demon was waiting for her just offshore. I blew up his boat, but I was too late—the demon had already called up a giant whale to swallow your mother— boat and all.

"But guess what—Henry escaped and swam back to me. *To me, son.* If Henry were a baby sea giant, wouldn't he have returned to his supposed parents? No, he swam back to *me*, because I'm the only father he's ever known. Henry doesn't belong in the ocean—he can't breathe underwater! And look at him—he's far too short to be a baby sea giant. My goodness, Bailey, if he were a baby sea giant, he'd be over a hundred feet tall by now, and even then he'd be considered a bit of a runt! No, my beautiful boy, I promise you, Henry is the same long-armed, blue-skinned Swiss troll you've always loved and you needn't worry yourself about this anymore. Henry is ours and no one else's. Don't let an evil lying demon make you feel guilty for a crime we never committed. Don't let anyone or *anything* turn you against me. I'm your father. I'm the one person who you can trust in this world, and that, my son, will always be the truth."

The spark on the oiled string was about to connect with the nitrocellulose.

"Have I answered your question, son?"

121

Bailey and Savannah, both eyeing the fuse, nervously nodded yes.

"Good," his father said, and he chucked the dynamite over his left shoulder.

Bailey and Savannah watched the stick arc through the gray beach town sky, spinning end over end.

Luckily, Henry did not think the stick of dynamite was a stick to be chased. He watched it fly and as it flew, he barked, *Roump?*

CHAPTER SEVENTEEN

THE TRUTH

MR. BOOM and his four thugs scrambled when they saw the dynamite hit the street and roll under his black truck.

"NO!" he yelled, ducking just moments before the dynamite exploded. The truck tipped over and lay on its side, crumpled, a gaping hole in its underside.

"RIP-ROARING RITA! YOU OWE ME A NEW TRUCK, DOUGIE!"

"I don't owe you anything, buddy!"

Cheri waved her fist up at him. "Dougie! Just what do you think you're doing? You can't throw dynamite into the middle of the street like that! We're trying to conduct honest business down here!"

"Cheri, don't forget who catches the faeries that raid your shop for fudge. Now, everybody, clear out!"

Savannah pointed her sword at Mr. Boom's crumpled

truck. "That bully in the winter coat has two birdcages. I think he's got faeries."

"I knew this was coming," Bailey's father muttered. "Kids, get the peanut-butter-honey mix and start rolling it into balls." Savannah did so, but Bailey could only look at Henry, who was wagging his tongue happily, just excited to be part of so much fun.

"No, Dad. I have to know the truth. There's too much evidence that Henry is a baby sea giant, and if that's true, then the right thing to do is to return him back to his parents."

"Son, we can't argue about this anymore. There are enemies at our gates. It's time to get on the same team and start rolling peanut-butter-honey balls."

But Bailey shook his head defiantly. "Dad, if I can prove without a doubt that Henry is a sea giant and not a troll, will you agree that we should bring Henry to his real home, even though it will be difficult, even though it will be dangerous, and even though we love him?"

His father sighed, then turned a bucket upside down and sat on it. "You're as stubborn as your mother, you know."

Bailey stood strong. "I just need the truth."

His father crossed his arms. "Okay, son. I guess we can't save ourselves until you have your say. I'm listening. Prove it. But if you *can't* prove it, then we drop this matter, and we *never* bring it up again. Agreed?"

Suddenly Bailey felt as nervous as he did in front of Mrs. Wood's seventh-grade class, but he knew the facts were on his side.

"All right, here goes. One: Trolls are hairy, even when they are babies, and Henry, already seven years old, doesn't have a hair on his entire body. Look, he doesn't even have eyebrows."

Bailey pointed to the smooth blue skin where eyebrows would normally be found, and Henry nodded excitedly and barked *roump!*

His father stroked his chin thoughtfully. "You are correct about that, but as I told your mother years ago, trolls can suffer alopecia just like humans. It is not hair that makes the man or the giant, Bailey."

Bailey was expecting that, so he moved on. "Two: You said that Henry isn't tall enough to be a baby sea giant. You said he'd have to be over a hundred feet tall by now if he was. Well, a lot of creatures can only grow as big as their environment allows them to. Dr. March talks about this in the introduction to his book. Before human civilization, giants roamed Earth and were as tall as mountains. We've kept Henry in a freezer for *seven years*. He can't grow even an inch taller as long as that's his home. Just like goldfish, iguanas, and dragons, if we keep him in a freezer, he will always be—even when he is fully grown—a runt. Now if we really loved Henry, we wouldn't want to stunt his growth, would we?"

With his arms still crossed, Bailey's father frowned, contemplating Henry's smiling, goofy face. He did love Henry, anyone could see that. And if you loved someone, whether troll or giant or human, why would you want to force him to be small?

"You make an interesting point, Bailey, but it's just your theory—not a proven fact."

It was time for Bailey's finale. While Savannah continued to roll peanut-butter-honey balls, he ran downstairs to his father's library. Behind the towering stacks of monster tomes, maps, and back issues of *Peculiar* stood a marble pedestal that displayed a brass salvage-diver's helmet that Bailey had often admired.

Fifty years ago, a cruel and vicious wereshark and his clan arrived on the shores of Whalefat Beach to claim the town for their own, threatening to turn every last one of its citizens into weresharks by biting them. Weresharks are human except when they come in contact with salt water, at which time they transform into horrifying, bloodthirsty creatures with shark heads, gills, and dorsal fins, but human bodies. Although this sounded like an exciting life change to some, most of Whalefat's citizens came to the Bucklebys to once again save them.

Bailey's grandfather, the brave and quite long-bearded Lawrence Buckleby, donned this very helmet and marched to the beach with his trusty spear. The wereshark and his clan were waiting for him, prepared to tear Bailey's grandfather to shreds and eat him. But Lawrence Buckleby challenged the leader to a duel—man to shark—in front of all of his clan. To save face, the wereshark leader had to accept, which improved Lawrence's odds considerably, since he only had to fight one wereshark instead of one hundred.

Lawrence Buckleby won that duel, most of which was

fought underwater. Their leader vanquished, the remaining weresharks swam away in defeat and shame. Lawrence gave his helmet to his young son, Dougie, to remind him that whenever the citizens of Whalefat Beach were threatened by monsters, it was up to the Bucklebys to muster the courage to protect them all.

Bailey hurried back to the roof with the helmet.

"And what do you propose to do with that?" his father asked with one eyebrow raised.

Bailey showed the helmet to Henry, who lowered his head as he had so many times for Bailey to place a sunhat on his head. He slid the helmet on, and although it was snug, Henry's head popped right in. Then Bailey removed the chickens from the bucket of ice water, and while standing on an upside down empty bucket, he slowly poured the water into the top of the helmet. As it filled, Henry smiled through the glass and barked *roump!*

His father stood up.

"Bailey, what are you doing? He'll drown!"

"Yes, he might. But you said Henry doesn't belong in the ocean because he can't breathe underwater. If he begins to turn blue—or bluer—then we'll take the helmet off. But if he doesn't—if he can breathe underwater—then I think even you, Dad, will have to admit that Henry is a baby sea giant."

Bailey kept pouring water into the helmet while his father and Savannah watched nervously. Henry didn't seem to mind at all, and even when the helmet was full, he barked cheerfully as bubbles rose from his nose and mouth.

Whole minutes went by, and it became clear to all of them that Henry was having no difficulty breathing. In fact, he seemed to quite like being submerged, barking happily while trying to bite the bubbles he was making. Bailey's father sat back down on the bucket, completely stunned, because his son had proven his point.

"Your mother was right. *You* were right. Our beautiful boy Henry is a sea giant after all—which makes *me* guilty of kidnapping."

His father put his head in his hands and began to cry, but Bailey jumped down and wrapped his arms around his father's huge chest.

"You didn't know, Dad. All you did was love Henry the best you could. There's no crime in that. But now you have to love him even harder—by letting him go."

His father looked at his son and wiped his eyes. He shrugged in defeat. "You've made me proud once again, Bailey. You always were better at monster classification than me. You're smart, you're kind, and you're brave enough to stand up to your old man. I do believe you're the greatest Buckleby of us all."

Bailey's eyes welled up with tears. His father squeezed his shoulders and it hurt in the best way. Henry gallomped over to them to lick both their faces, but the glass of the diver's helmet blocked his tongue.

"Thank you, buddy," his father said quietly, pulling the helmet off Henry's head, allowing the water to splash all over them—which Henry licked right off his face.

"Okay, boy, okay! You know I love you, too."

"We can't stay on this roof, Dad," Bailey insisted. "We have to do the right thing and return Henry to his parents. That's the *only* way we can stop all this."

Savannah peered over the side. "I think we're going to have to deal with those two crazy faeries first."

Bailey looked, too. Mr. Boom had opened the two cage doors to release his two well-trained faeries, who shot out and up into the air, mad and hungry.

CHAPTER EIGHTEEN

DO NOT EAT THAT FAERY

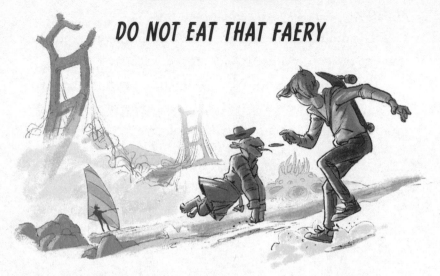

BAILEY'S FATHER YELLED, "Here they come, kids. Throw the peanut butter balls!"

The two trained killers rose up three stories and hovered above the roof.

"They're wearing little suits," Savannah gasped.

The twelve-inch-tall monsters were indeed wearing leather faery-sized battle gear, holes cut in the back to allow their chitin wings to poke through and spread wide. Mr. Boom appreciated attire designed to inspire fear, but the old-fashioned football headgear they wore served another function, too—to protect them from Frisbees.

"Peanut butter! Peanut butter!" Bailey's father shouted, and though he was a rotund man, he could move quickly when he wanted to, running from one end of the Buckleby roof to the other like a shortstop, chucking peanut-butter-honey baseballs at the faeries in rapid fire.

One-eyed orange tiger-stripe and yellow-breasted Bill Collector ducked and dodged. Their new owner had been starving them of sugar to make them hungry and mean. The smell of the peanut-butter-honey mix nearly overpowered them. Bill couldn't help but watch each sugar-packed ball fall to the street below.

When Bill Collector's head turned for a moment too long, Savannah nailed him straight in the chest.

Sweet, sweet honey. Bill Collector began to lick and bite at his leather suit, soon ripping it to shreds. In his distraction, he forgot about the enemy and floated downward to the street.

"GET BACK UP THERE, BILL!" boomed Mr. Boom through the megaphone. But Bill Collector was crazed with sugar lust and dove for more peanut-butter-honey.

One-Eye could not be so easily tempted. He snarled, his bloodshot eye growing bigger as he revealed all five fingernails that he planned to use as knives on his former captor's face.

Dougie beckoned Bailey to come closer. "Son, I think this would be a good time—"

But Bailey was one step ahead of him. He had a Frisbee in each hand and whipped them through the air. *Pft* and *Pft!*

Both discs beaned One-Eye square in the forehead, but One-Eye's leather helmet did its job. Instead of slowing him, the Frisbee hits only amplified the faery's anger. The pint-sized orange killer fluttered toward them, his tattered wings buzzing. Then he zoomed in.

Bailey's father was agile, but not fast enough for an angry faery with a vendetta. Savannah picked up her sword and took a swing as One-Eye went charging by.

Bailey's father stopped her. "No, orphan girl, please don't hurt him."

One-Eye pulled a fake, put his feet out at the last minute, and stretched out his clawed toes to pluck out Dougie's eyes.

Roump, roump . . . WHARP.

Bailey's father looked between his nine fingers. Henry sat on his haunches in front of him with One-Eye caught firmly in his mouth.

"*He did it,*" Bailey said proudly. "Henry caught him in midair! He's never caught a seagull before, but he caught the faery just like a Frisbee!"

"Good boy," Bailey's father said calmly. "You're a good sweet boy, but, Henry, DO NOT EAT THAT FAERY."

Bailey's father reached for One-Eye, but like a golden retriever who doesn't want the tug-of-war game to end, Henry pulled his blue head back so that his master couldn't grab his new toy.

"Henry, boy, that's a fine specimen of a faery—an orange-striped beauty. Don't eat him."

Henry wagged his head back and forth, shaking One-Eye vigorously as the faery lashed out with sharp finger-nails and toenails, trying to scrape away Henry's face and get him to loosen his grip. But Henry's sea-giant skin was too thick to be penetrated, and he jumped up and down on all fours, barking with a full mouth of faery, "*Wharp, wharp, WHARP!*"

"I know what to do," Savannah said. "I'll swap him a chicken."

"Good thinking, orphan girl. Henry will drop anything for his dinner."

Savannah took a raw chicken from their supplies and wagged it in front of Henry. "Dinner, boy?" Sure enough, Henry released One-Eye in exchange for the chicken, while Bailey's father grabbed the faery by its neck, stuffed him into his canvas bag, and duct-taped it shut.

"You belong to the Bucklebys once again, my one-eyed beauty!"

Savannah peered over the edge of the steel fortress. "That bald-headed bully in the winter coat has a new friend."

CHAPTER NINETEEN

THE FAMOUS LABYRINTHIAN OF THE MOJAVE DESERT

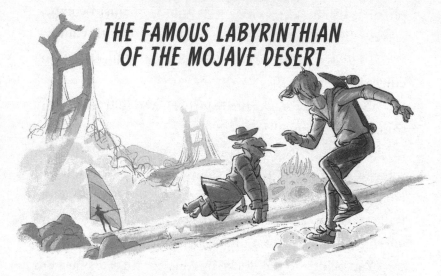

A SEVEN-FOOT-TALL BEAST paced nervously below. Hair sprouted between the buttons of a cotton work shirt much too small for him. He had the head of a bull with eyes wide apart and two white horns that curved up to the sky ending in black razor tips. The creature cracked his knuckles and kept pushing his shirt flaps into his jeans to maintain a respectable appearance. His steel-tipped leather boots had to be the largest size ever made, and they were well scuffed, like he'd done plenty of steel-tipped kicking. He looked entirely uncomfortable in his clothes and seemed like he'd rather be anywhere but Whalefat Beach.

"Is that a minotaur?" Bailey asked. He'd never seen one in real life, though he'd read plenty about them.

"A bullhead? I bet he's a descendant of the Bullhead Brigade, too!" Savannah shouted, raising her sword in the air.

"Ah! You're a student of true American history, orphan girl," Bailey's father said approvingly. "Fine warriors, the Bullhead Brigade. Although this minotaur must be experiencing hard times if he's thrown in his lot with Candycane Boom. But we are Bucklebys and will fight any monster that might oppose us."

Mr. Boom shouted through his megaphone: "You're up next, Nikos. *Don't* disappoint me."

As the minotaur stepped into the middle of the street, he gave his bald employer a look as if he didn't like his kind at all. Nikos carried a very large rusted chain at the end of which was an anchor at least four feet in length, quite capable of mooring a yacht. In an impressive show of strength, he started swinging the anchor and chain in a great circle, and then hurled it toward the roof. Bailey and Savannah had to jump out of the way for fear of being crushed. The anchor hooked one of the pulleys and stuck fast.

Bailey's father tried to lift it off, but the anchor was too heavy, even for him. The minotaur held the chain tight, and then, hand over hand, started to climb *up* the steel plank wall.

"What do you think you're doing, friend?" Dougie shouted down.

The minotaur grunted as he took one slow step after another. "Climbing your wall."

"Who are *you*?" Bailey asked.

"Nikos Tekton—the famous Labyrinthian of the Mojave Desert," he said. Bailey's father tried again to lift the anchor, but to no avail.

"I've never heard of you," Bailey's father shouted down.

The minotaur paused in his ascent. "Surely you have! Minotaurs have lived in the Mojave Desert for two hundred years and have built the most magnificent mazes ever seen. We are a frequent travel destination for those humans who believe we are real. I named my labyrinth the *Lost Hoplite,* and it is more complicated than any maze you will find."

Bailey's father shouted back, "Labyrinths are those things where you intentionally get yourself lost and then try to find your way back to where you started, right?"

As the minotaur climbed, he snorted in frustration. "Labyrinths are an important part of Western culture. They challenge the mind in beautiful ways. Have you heard of the Reignac-Sur-Indre in France? Or perhaps the Maze at Ashcombe in Australia?"

"No, buddy," Bailey's father said. "I haven't, but could you stop climbing my wall, please?"

The minotaur paused briefly. "You must have heard of the labyrinth of ancient Greece that Theseus entered to wage his legendary battle with the greatest minotaur ever known—my ancestor Asterion?"

His father shrugged. "No, I haven't, and honestly, you think too highly of yourself. To me you're just another thug threatening my family."

Putting one hand in front of the other, Nikos Tekton continued to make progress. "I admit, we don't receive as many customers as we would like. Our location is a bit too remote for humans. Unfortunately, I had to borrow money from some unscrupulous men to complete my maze's construction, requiring me to take on additional and often dishonorable employment. But I am dedicated to my art."

"Pottery is better," Bailey's father shouted.

"Pottery is for simpletons!"

Dougie chuckled to himself. "Everybody loves a good pot, buddy. You wouldn't be strong-arming for a loan shark if you had gone into pottery."

The minotaur only answered with a snort and continued to climb.

Bailey's father looked at his son with fierce determination. "We can't budge this anchor and he's almost here. We have to dynamite him."

Bailey shook his head. "No, Dad. We can't solve all our problems with explosives."

"Bailey," his father sighed. "As you grow older, you'll learn that sometimes—when you've exhausted all other options—a good stick of dynamite is the only thing that will save you—"

Suddenly the minotaur leapt over the side of the roof, boots first, and gave Dougie Buckleby two steel-toed boots right to the forehead. He fell like a bag of bricks. Nikos leaned over and offered him his hand.

"Come on, Mr. Buckleby. Upsy-daisy. I hit you pretty hard there."

Bailey's father sat up, but he seemed a bit confused. His eyes were rolling around in his head. "What day is it? Is it yesterday?"

"No," Nikos said calmly. "It's Monday."

"So it's tomorrow, then," Mr. Buckleby said with relief, and then fell back on his elbows, out of commission.

The minotaur clicked his bull tongue. "I must apologize, children, but Candycane Boom hired me to help him obtain the baby sea giant by removing your father as an obstacle."

"He's not *my* father," Savannah screamed, raising her sword. "But *you're* gonna wish you hadn't messed with *us!*"

"Wait," Bailey said, trying to keep cool, even though his father had most likely suffered a very bad concussion. He knew he couldn't best the huge and muscled minotaur in strength, so he tried very hard not to get angry, to think carefully, and to formulate a plan.

"My father may not have heard of Asterion and the history of the minotaurs, but I have," Bailey said cautiously, recalling page 110 of his favorite book. "I know that minotaurs value their honor more than anything else, and that the greatest possible honor they can earn is by victory in one-on-one combat."

The minotaur nodded in agreement. "Yes, that is true, although we prefer our duels to be held in the center of a labyrinth. Sadly, I haven't been in a labyrinth in years, but Mr. Boom has hired me to do a job, and although he is not an honorable man himself, I intend to complete my contract with him."

"Over our dead bodies," Savannah said, narrowing her eyes.

Nikos Tekton shook his great bull head. Bailey could see his beard was ragged and loose, even though Dr. March's book told him that minotaurs were very proud of their beards and kept them tied neatly together with gold rings. Bailey suspected this minotaur had to pawn his gold beard rings long ago.

He spoke carefully. "I offer you a duel, sir. Whoever falls to the ground first loses, and the winner takes Henry."

Henry wagged his tongue and barked *roump!* Nikos eyed the big blue baby, pulling on his ragged beard as he considered the offer. "It's a tempting proposal. Your offer *would* allow me to honor my contract to Mr. Boom *and* circumvent me from doing any fatal harm to children *and* allow me the honor of one-on-one combat against a clearly formidable foe."

The minotaur studied Bailey carefully. Bailey waited, not sure what he would do if the minotaur refused. But Nikos finally extended his hand. "Your offer is fair, Bailey Buckleby. How shall we begin?"

CHAPTER TWENTY

AN HONORABLE DUEL

THERE WAS A light spread of gravel on the rooftop, and Bailey had always wondered why it was there. When he was younger and used to walk toward the edge of the roof with his eyes closed, he would listen to it crunch under his shoes and wonder, *Did someone used to have a rock garden up here?* At the edge of the roof, there was a slightly raised and slanted plastic trim all around the perimeter, for decoration mostly, but also to allow the rain to slide off and not collect on the roof. Even with his eyes closed, Bailey could feel when there was no gravel beneath his shoes and where the plastic perimeter began, alerting him that he was very, very close to falling three stories down.

As he watched the sun dip past the horizon of the Pacific, and the whole Monday evening became a little dimmer, Bailey hoped that this knowledge would give him a slight advantage. He stalled so it could get even darker.

"I'd like to go get a few more Frisbees for our battle," Bailey said.

"Be my guest," Nikos said, bowing. "I have heard that you are a fine Frisbee thrower, so I would expect that to be your weapon of choice."

"What will yours be?" Bailey asked.

Nikos tapped both of his horns. "These are all I need. They are quite sharp, but I promise not to purposely impale you. We agreed that whoever falls to the ground loses, correct? Those are the words you chose."

"Yes," Bailey agreed, letting out a nervous breath. "No one need be impaled."

"I'd prefer my horns not be responsible for your death," Nikos said calmly. "Please go fetch the Frisbees you need, but do not dilly-dally."

"Are we in the Amazon?" Bailey's father asked, holding his head in both hands.

"No, Mr. Buckleby," Savannah said, and decided she shouldn't tell him any more.

Bailey went down to his tower of Frisbees next to the register in the front room and grabbed seven red discs and a flashlight. Then he walked slowly up the staircase to the hatch that led to the roof. The longer he delayed, the darker it would be, which would give him a critical advantage over the minotaur. Also, he didn't want to rush his death.

When he stepped out onto the gravel of the rooftop, he heard Mr. Boom's voice through the megaphone. "WHISTLING WENDY, WHAT'S TAKING SO LONG UP THERE?"

The minotaur did not need anything to help raise the volume of his voice. He shouted back, "The boy and I are about to have a duel of honor."

"I DIDN'T PAY YOU TO DUEL!"

Nikos shouted back, "You haven't paid me anything yet, sir, so be patient!"

Bailey looked over the side of the roof and saw Candycane Boom and the four sophomores staring up at them.

"Are you ready, Bailey?" Nikos asked.

Bailey nodded yes and gave the flashlight to Savannah.

"Please be careful, Bailey," she said, looking worried. "Bullheads have the strength of ten humans and are easily angered."

He smiled and whispered, "Just shine this flashlight on my Frisbees when we begin."

Savannah nodded.

Bailey backed up as far as he dared toward the roof's edge until he felt the plastic trim beneath his feet. With only a crescent moon and a few stars in the night sky, there was very little light left.

Bailey started to spin two Frisbees vertically, one on each index finger, the other five in his hoodie pocket. He weaved them back and forth, one over the other, as Nikos snorted and kicked gravel with his boots, getting ready to charge. Bailey nodded to Savannah and she shone the light.

As Bailey spun the Frisbees and Savannah pointed the light at them, all Nikos could see in front of him was a hypnotic, spinning red glow. Page 110 of *In the Shadow of Monsters* had also taught him that minotaurs, like their bull relatives, were easily hypnotized and angered by the color red. Nikos stopped snorting and kicking for a moment and stared.

"Please don't do that," the minotaur said. "It's very distracting."

Bailey whipped one of the red Frisbees in between Nikos's bull eyes. *Pft!*

"*Grrr!*" the minotaur yelled, infuriated. He charged, but just as he reached his opponent, Bailey darted to the right, keeping two spinning red illuminated Frisbees in front of Nikos. The minotaur stopped himself just before running off the roof, and Bailey skipped backward blindly until he felt the plastic edge of the roof beneath his feet.

Nikos snorted. "I see what you are trying to do, young Buckleby, but I'm no simpleton."

Bailey said nothing. He kept the red Frisbees spinning while Savannah lit them up with the flashlight.

"*Grrr!*" Nikos charged again with his fist cocked, but he couldn't focus on anything but the red Frisbees, so when Bailey sidestepped again at the last minute, the minotaur kept charging forward, again nearly falling off the edge of the roof as he slipped on the gravel. As he went by,

Bailey knocked him on the head with three Frisbees. *Pft, Pft,* and *Pft!*

Bailey skipped backward and took his original position at the other end of the roof, this time at the very edge so his heels hung over the side. If he lost his balance or the ocean wind picked up, he would likely fall three stories to the street. He started to spin the Frisbees again, knowing he only had one left in his pocket.

"Bailey Buckleby—" Nikos growled, but he couldn't concentrate with the red Frisbees spinning in front of him. The minotaur charged again, but just as his horns nearly pierced Bailey's stomach, Bailey zipped all three Frisbees into his opponent's forehead—*Pft, Pft,* and *Pft!*

Momentum carried Nikos forward, and he would have surely plunged to his death or at least very serious injury if Bailey hadn't turned quickly and grabbed the minotaur's belt with both hands.

"Savannah, help me!"

She ran over and grabbed the minotaur's belt, too, as he stood on the edge of the roof, waving his arms frantically, trying to regain his balance.

"HOLY HOPPING HANNAH, WHAT'S GOING ON UP THERE?" Mr. Boom yelled through the megaphone.

Bailey feared that the floundering minotaur would pull him and Savannah over the side. But finally, they pulled him back in time for him to steady himself. The minotaur dropped to one knee.

"I nearly fell," the minotaur gasped.

"But you didn't," Savannah said proudly. "So you should thank us, Mr. Bullhead!"

The minotaur stood up, towering over them, and snorted. Even by the crescent moon, Bailey could see he was angry and quite capable of tearing them into multiple parts. But Nikos extended his large hand so that he could shake Bailey's and congratulate him.

"I do thank you, not only for a fair and honorable fight, but for saving my life. I am in debt to you both. I must admit, you are quick on your feet, young Buckleby."

"Not quick enough to beat me at Four Square." Savannah grinned.

"It was a good duel," Bailey agreed.

"Now that I have been defeated honorably, I must suggest you find a new location to hide your baby sea giant—Candycane Boom is determined to acquire him. He has a buyer who will pay quite handsomely for him."

Down below, Mr. Boom had long since lost his patience. "Bring that sea giant down here, NOW!"

"I won't," Nikos yelled back. "The boy and I had an honorable duel, and he won fairly."

"NOW, YOU DISOBEDIENT COW!"

"I don't think Mr. Boom intends to leave," Bailey said.

"No, he doesn't," Nikos said, shaking his bull head. "And I don't suppose he will pay me for my efforts, either. But I can admit to you now that Axel Pazuzu had two plans of attack prepared."

Savannah stood on an overturned bucket to grab Nikos by the left horn. "What do you mean, *two plans*?"

Nikos cleared his throat to regain his composure. "At this very moment, goblins are tunneling into your back room. They intend to overwhelm you and take Henry for themselves. They are working with Axel, too."

Savannah gasped and immediately dove down the stairs.

"Hey, wait for me!" Bailey yelled after her. "It's not safe for you down there alone!"

"Stop her, young Buckleby," Nikos said urgently. "There are more goblins beneath the earth than you realize."

Bailey's father sat up, looked around at an imaginary crowd, and asked, "Is it my turn to speak? This doesn't look like the Las Vegas Monster Hunters Conference at all!"

Henry licked Bailey's father's face happily and barked *roump, roump, roump!*

"Please watch my father and Henry," Bailey said as he hurried down the stairs and caught up with Savannah in the back room. She already had her sword raised, ready to bring it down in a swift, deadly chop on whatever threat lay in front of her.

"They're trying to trick us, but we're smarter than them," she whispered.

Bailey had only known Savannah as the loudest girl in Mrs. Wood's classroom, and he'd never heard her voice so quiet and serious before. He sidestepped softly around her, keeping his back to the wall and gripping one of the red Frisbees between his thumb and finger.

"Savannah, just step back. The goblins are coming for us and we don't know how many there are."

"They're already here," she whispered, pointing at a gaping hole surrounded by torn-up linoleum and dirt where the goblins' cages had once sat. Canopus and Capella had dug their way to freedom, and now Savannah, just a few feet from the tunnel, stared intently at a clear Ziploc bag filled with shining gold nuggets. A long piece of twine uncoiled from the bag into the hole, which led down into the darkness. The bag of gold was slowly creeping, inch by inch, toward the hole, like bait for a fish.

Savannah was the fish.

"Step back from the bag, Savannah. *The goblins are right there.*"

Her sword rose higher. "I know," she whispered, swinging the sword down and chopping the twine in half, releasing the bag of gold, which she grabbed and held up in the air.

"We're rich, Bailey!" she screamed in victory, turning to him with a huge glowing smile. But it was short-lived, because suddenly a bright light shone from the hole, growing more and more dazzling, blinding them both.

A voice growled: "Star light, star bright, we respect your power and your might!"

Then Bailey felt a painful thunk on the back of his head, and he crumpled to the ground.

CHAPTER TWENTY-ONE

WE VOW WE WILL GIVE YOU BACK THE NIGHT

BAILEY WOKE WITH a splitting headache in a bouncing cage made of white plastic piping tied together with nylon rope, rusty bicycle chains, and copper wire. The make-shift cage bobbed up and down in time with six marching goblins who struggled underneath the weight. The pipes jutted out from all sides, and because the tunnel they walked through had been dug by two-foot-tall goblins, there wasn't much spare space for a seventh-grader-sized cage, so the pipes frequently stuck against the tunnel walls, causing the goblin guards to have to stop and tilt the cage to the left or right to keep moving. Bailey sat up and saw he wasn't the only one imprisoned—Savannah sat in her own cage carried by six more goblins just ahead of him.

Bailey checked his pockets. No luck—his phone was gone, as was the Frisbee that he kept in his secret hoodie pocket. They even took his belt, which might have proved useful for a possible breakout.

He figured he and Savannah had been taken deep underground into one of the legendary goblin tunnels he had read about in *In the Shadow of Monsters*. He wondered how long he had been unconscious and how far down into the tunnels they had traveled.

It would be totally reasonable for a twelve-year-old girl in this situation to fear being dismembered, disemboweled, dissected, or even eaten, but if Savannah Mistivich worried about such fates she did not show it. She stood on the tips of her toes and reached her slender hand through a crack in the piping so she could run her fingers along the dirt ceiling as they marched along.

She saw Bailey was awake. "Hey, Bailey boy," she whispered. "How you feeling?" She winked and wiggled her fingers as they dragged along the dirt ceiling, but Bailey couldn't guess what she was up to.

He grabbed two of the plastic cage bars and gave them a good shake. They were securely tied with chain and wire. His father might have been strong enough to pull the pipes apart, but not Bailey.

"Don't shake the cage," one of the goblins snapped. Bailey sat down to calm himself. Without a weapon, he could only rely on his words, so he considered what he said next very carefully.

"Which one of you is in charge? I have an offer."

"I'm in charge," Capella said, "and we're not interested in any of your human tricks."

"She's not in charge, but she's right—no trickery," Canopus said.

Capella hoisted her corner of the cage up higher and snapped back, "I'm certainly more in charge than you, Canopus! Who let themselves be captured by the humans and nearly got us both sold into slavery?"

Canopus raised his head higher. "It was all part of my master plan, wasn't it? And now we have *two* human prisoners to bargain with."

The goblins at the back corners of the cage started chuckling quietly.

"Shut up back there!" Capella barked.

"Don't tell them to shut up," Canopus said.

"They were laughing at you, my dear."

"No, they were laughing at the situation."

"*You're* the situation!"

The other goblins snickered, obviously trying to keep from laughing out loud.

Bailey tried to be as patient as possible. "Listen, I know you're probably very upset that we locked you up in cages, but you have to understand that our customer was scared of you, and we didn't realize that you think the lights you were stealing are stars—anyways, I want to make you an offer that will make you the richest monsters in the world."

Now all the goblins let loose laughing.

"You'll soon see, human boy, that we goblins have all the gold we could ever need, which is none at all," Capella said. "Mr. Pazuzu and humans may worship gold, but we serve far higher and nobler masters—the stars."

"Bailey, look, she's right!" Savannah said in awe, pointing at the walls of the tunnel, which were gradually become larger, smoother, and brighter as they marched along. The tunnels enlarged into halls warmly glowing with torchlight, each torch held in place with a clamp made of pure gold. Beneath them were slabs of gold worn smooth by goblin feet. From the ceiling, large crude gold hooks held gold bowls of oil that burned and provided more light.

"*So much gold*," Savannah whispered in awe.

All twelve goblins chuckled.

"You probably want a gold necklace for your long, ugly neck," one of the goblins chided her.

"And you probably want gold rings for all your hairless fingers," another hissed.

"You probably want to wear as much gold as you can until you couldn't even walk!" said another one whose face had so many boils, Savannah couldn't tell where his eyes and nose were.

"Gold doesn't even have a very pretty color. Why would you want to wear it at all?" a tiny female goblin guard asked, and Bailey did see that although all the goblins wore plenty of jewelry, not one piece was gold. They wore painted stone necklaces, and iron bracelets, and collars that were once plastic key chains. One goblin had pierced his ear with so many safety pins, Bailey couldn't even count them.

"Gold shines because it is cursed with evil magic," Capella informed them matter-of-factly. "It drives all monsters to madness—*especially humans*. If they knew how much gold was down here, they would probably dig and dig and ruin everything in their path to take it all and cover themselves in it, from their funny-looking heads to their disgusting stubby toes."

"They would," said one of the goblins in the back.

"They surely would," said another.

"They *definitely* would," said another. "And they'd destroy *our* homes without a second thought."

"Yes," Canopus said. "But we will turn that greed against them and save the stars."

All the goblins bellowed in squeaky unison, "To the Eighteenth Goblin Order of Star Guardians!"

Capella tugged on Bailey's hoodie to show him her necklace of stones that shone a bright metallic goldlike color. "I like the color myself," she said. "But these stones are fool's gold. It's a much healthier mineral to use— completely magic-free."

Again Bailey wondered how these creatures who were smart enough to build all these tunnels could believe in such ridiculous things as fallen stars and evil gold magic. But then he had to admit that most humans he knew would do just about anything for even the tiniest chunk of gold. Maybe these goblins were right after all.

The goblins marched on, only occasionally complaining about Bailey's and Savannah's weight. Bailey realized that the tunnel was gradually sloping downward. He had to pop his ears twice and feared that they were miles beneath the earth. As they took turn after turn, Bailey knew that if he were to escape, he'd have no idea which way to go.

"*Pst!* Bailey boy! Look!"

Savannah opened her hands to reveal a whole collection of stones, many of them small chunks of gold. She sat cross-legged in the middle of her cage, cupping her hands, and slowly, methodically, started sharpening the two biggest stones against each other.

"Your girlfriend's plots are useless," Canopus said to Bailey, and he feared the goblin was right again.

Hours passed and anxiety kept Bailey from sleeping. Even though he had been told they were to be ransomed, he feared that if he went to sleep, these goblins would slit his throat. He felt awful that he had brought Savannah into this mess. She was by far the strongest and bravest kid he knew, but she might also have been the loneliest. Her parents never came to Parents' Day, she had no siblings, and other girls often made fun of her for being so tough. Bailey knew his father had to be worried he was gone, but would anyone worry about Savannah? Maybe she was so strong, even loneliness could not beat her.

He listened to Savannah scraping and scraping. Bailey had to figure a way to talk them out of this dilemma.

The tunnel opened into three passageways, and their guards took the middle one. Other goblins began to squeeze by them, many of them carrying electrical wiring and power strips. The goblin chatter was high, and as they passed they greeted Bailey and Savannah's captors with "Hello!" and "A Good Day to Be Goblin to You!"

The tunnels crisscrossed and were labeled with signs like HEAVEN'S HIGHWAY and KEEPER'S BOULEVARD. The one they were marching down now had a wooden sign that read STARLIGHT SANCTUARY NORTH END, and the farther they marched, the brighter the tunnel became.

The goblins put their cages down, and others stopped to peer and poke at the human prisoners.

"What do they eat?"

"You know what they eat. *Anything.* Blood, ice, the milk of any mother of any species."

"Oh, that's just foul!"

"Foul indeed. Don't put your fingers in the cages. Humans bite them off."

Their goblin guards were putting on shaded goggles. In front of Savannah's cage, two of them raised a huge spotlight that was twice their size. Three goblins from down the tunnel rushed forward with an extension cord that seemed to unravel forever. A power strip was connected to the end in one of the goblins' hands. As she approached, the goblin knelt down on her right knee.

"Star of the night, I offer you light."

Savannah's guards replied, "This rescued star accepts your light."

With heads bowed, the guards presented the plug of the spotlight to their fellow goblin, who held her palms out. She took the plug carefully, ceremoniously, kissed it lightly, and plugged it in. The spotlight blazed brilliantly, and Bailey then knew this was the light the goblins had used to blind them in the back room.

The goblins without goggles were mesmerized and immediately put into a trance. The adjoining tunnels filled with goblins who hummed with reverence at the bright star, here in their presence, under the earth instead of high above it. They chanted in unison:

"Star so bright, you give us light, we vow we will give you back the night!"

Canopus could barely look away, even with shaded goggles on.

Capella turned to Bailey and said, "You should count yourself fortunate. You are about to see what no human has ever seen before. We are about to enter the greatest achievement of all the Goblin Orders—the Starlight Sanctuary."

Their guards picked up their cages while two more joined their train to carry the bright spotlight. Then they marched forward through a grand gold entrance into the largest underground chamber Bailey had ever seen or could ever imagine.

CHAPTER TWENTY-TWO

LAMPS, LAMPS, LAMPS

BAILEY WISHED Dr. Frederick March and his father could see this. If the two hunters could agree on anything, it would be that this room was stunning monster ingenuity. The mammoth cave extended so far, Bailey could not see the end of it, even though it was incredibly well lit. Christmas tree lights dangled from the ceiling, wrapped around stalactites that dripped into silent pools. There were hundreds of electrical lights, if not thousands. White and red and green and every other color, too. Reading lamps sat on every available rock. Headlights without cars attached to them had been carefully set in circles surrounding stalagmites and beautiful geodes. Around these minerals stood spotlights that fired their beams toward the cave ceiling high above. Fluorescent light tubes had been stacked into pyramids, globes intended for ceiling fans had been stacked into cubes, lamps without lampshades to hinder their glory stood in formation for hundreds of feet. All blazed bright, filling the cave with light.

The goblins carried Bailey and Savannah into the great chamber where hundreds of other goblins knelt in prayer, all wearing shaded goggles. Many of them wore tiny white robes that looked to be human T-shirts stitched crudely together. Goblins with white robes and white gloves were carefully polishing the lamps with men's business socks. Bailey wondered which department store manager had come in one morning to find his entire underwear display gone along with all the store lights, with no evidence of a break-in except a freshly burrowed hole through the tile floor.

The goblins set the cages down in the center of a circle of stage lights, which blazed directly at Bailey and Savannah, burning their eyes and making Bailey realize just how tired he was.

Canopus gave Bailey's cage a good kick.

"Now you know, human boy, what it's like to be the one in the cage."

Capella showed more compassion. "I would give you dinner, but we don't have human food here," she said.

"I can hear a waterfall. Could we have fresh water at least?" Bailey asked, feeling parched, trying to remember sixth-grade human biology, during which he might have learned how long the human body could survive without water.

"That's not a waterfall. Those are the bicycles. But I will bring you water from one of the pools."

Bailey looked in the direction of the roaring sound. It was coming from the other side of a row of streetlamps. Between them he saw rows and rows of stationary bicycles, and on each one a goblin pedaled furiously. In unison, their pedaling did sound like the roar of a waterfall. From each bicycle flowed a thick black cable, which all joined to a thicker black cable, which snaked to the center of the Starlight Sanctuary and connected to a large black machine, which could only be a generator. From the generator flowed many smaller cables, which broke into power strips, which fed all the lights with electricity.

"Mr. Pazuzu is greedy for gold just like you humans, but he has proven useful to our mission. He taught us how to transform our love into star food, and he has promised that he will help us put the stars back into the sky."

"You mean electricity," Bailey said. "That generator is converting your energy into electricity."

"No—*star food*. The stars need our love or they die," Capella insisted.

"Those lights aren't stars. They're man-made devices being lit by electricity created by that man-made generator."

Capella shook her head and closed her eyes. "You humans are so arrogant, you think you've created everything. I'll get your water."

As Capella left, a dozen goblins ventured closer to their cages with sticks in their hands. They prodded Bailey and

Savannah at a safe distance, looking for proof of what they had heard—that humans could shoot small stones from their fingertips so fast they could split a goblin's head open and kill him instantly.

"Show us your fingers, human boy. Show us your fingers, human girl."

Bailey opened his hands, which were empty. He looked over at Savannah's cage. Her long black hair was ratty from sweat and dirt that had fallen from the tunnel roof that she had disturbed with her fingertips. Bailey feared she would open her hands to reveal two sharpened stones. They would surely kill her if she did, but her hands were empty.

"Cast a spell for us, human. Show us magic."

"Humans aren't magical," Bailey explained. "We're just good at science."

"Show us *science*, then," one of the ugliest goblins garbled. He had large boils that erupted from half of his nose.

Bailey pointed to the furiously pedaling goblins on the bicycles. "There's science right there—you're creating electricity with biomechanical energy."

The crowd of goblins looked confused for a moment, and then a wave of anger overtook them. "Blasphemy! Liar! Human wickedness! How dare you insult the stars that give us life and beauty? The bicycles transform our *love* into light. Mr. Pazuzu told us so."

Capella returned with two bowls of water.

"Leave the humans alone. They are children. If you scare them to death, they will be of no use to us."

Bailey and Savannah accepted the bowls of water through the bars of their cages. The water stunk like rotten eggs but at least it was clear. There were no bugs in this cave, so Bailey reasoned that it was probably okay to drink. Then he reasoned his science was maybe not so accurate. Then he reasoned he had no choice.

He drank the water and then crouched down to Capella's level. "What if I could lead you to a thousand more stars waiting to be freed?" Bailey was thinking of Lamps, Lamps, Lamps, the home lighting outlet on Oceanview Boulevard that guaranteed to satisfy all your home lighting needs. "If you free us, we will help you save them."

"Don't try your human trickery on us, boy. We are doing just fine rescuing the stars on our own. We estimate we are more than halfway done."

"What?" Bailey said, sitting up. "You can't be serious. Do you know how many fallen stars there are in the world?"

"Seven hundred and sixty-five thousand, four hundred and forty-two," Capella said, quite matter-of-factly.

Bailey smiled, but Capella was not joking.

"You can't really think so," Bailey insisted. "Whether you think they are stars or electrical lights, you must know that there are millions of them in California alone."

"I stand by our elders' calculations. Now be quiet and take a nap. We rest here for a short while and then we continue our march to the great open sea."

Bailey did not like the sound of that. "What will you do with us when we reach the great open sea?"

Capella grinned proudly with sharp fangs curling out over her bottom lip.

"We will trade you to your father for the baby sea giant and return him to his crib at the bottom of the sea. If your father doesn't agree, we give you and the girl to the sea giants so they can eat you to avenge the kidnapping of their son. In either case, we expect their gratitude. They are the only creatures alive who are tall enough to lift the stars to the sky and restore the heavens to their former glory. The Eighteenth Goblin Order of Star Guardians will have succeeded where the seventeen orders before us failed, and we will live under beautiful starlight once more."

Savannah whispered to Bailey through the bars. "Bailey boy, these goblins are cuckoo for Cocoa Puffs."

CHAPTER TWENTY-THREE

COME BACK TO ME, BOY

THE GOBLINS kept the stars lit all night with constant pedaling. Bailey couldn't sleep, despite his weariness, because even with his eyes closed, the thousands of light-bulbs blazed and formed red and yellow spots against his eyelids. All he could do was watch the goblins diligently cycling, changing shifts every thirty minutes, while others in miniature T-shirt robes knelt in prayer before the bulbs that still more goblins polished continuously.

But eventually, like Savannah in the cage next to him, sleep overtook him. His head rested on one arm while he used the other to shield his eyes from the cave's brilliant and unnatural light.

He thought of his mother—or maybe he dreamed of her—somewhere across the ocean, alive somehow, living inside a whale like the original Whalefatians had, with a tattered and wet copy of *In the Shadow of Monsters*. Bailey envisioned her studying the book furiously, looking for clues as to how she could escape and come home.

"Mom, Mom!" he called out, but the goblin guard whose back rested against Bailey's cage banged on the bars with the back of his hand. "Your mother isn't here, boy. Go back to sleep."

Maybe he did, because it seemed only a second later that he heard a light scratching against the plastic piping. He opened his aching eyes and remembered where he was.

Scratch, scratch, scratch.

Bailey rolled on his belly and saw a familiar little face.

It was like a rat's but slightly bigger, with two tusks protruding over its upper lip. It cocked its head at Bailey in greeting. Amazed, he realized it was one of their ratatoskers, and sure enough, a piece of loose-leaf paper had been folded and refolded and pierced on the little creature's right tusk. Bailey pulled it off gently so as not to disturb his goblin jailers. He unfolded it and read:

Bailey, my beautiful boy:
I know you're alive because you're just too smart to be defeated by a bunch of pea-brained tunnel goblins. I'm too big to get through the tunnel, so I tried to expand the entrance with dynamite, but that only caused a complete collapse. I'm sure you are lost underground, so I sent this ratatosker to find you. Keep him close, and when the time is right, let him sniff the attached cloth. It's from my sweatshirt. He will pick up my scent and run to me. Follow him. Come back to me, boy.

Be safe down there. I love you,
Dad

Sure enough, a tiny piece of red cloth, stained with pizza sauce, was taped to the letter.

The ratatosker sat up on its hind legs and lifted its nose in the air as if it sensed it was time for a mission. It raised one four-toed paw.

"First we have to get out of these cages," Bailey whispered. "But I don't know how to do that."

But Savannah did. She was pretending to sleep on her belly, her head on one arm while her other hand methodically, slowly scraped away at the extension cord the goblins had used to bind the piping that made the floor of her cage. She had hidden away the two sharpened stones in her hoodie after all. Bailey felt very lucky, for if they couldn't talk their way out of this dilemma, they would have to fight their way out, and if his father wasn't available, Savannah was quickly proving herself to be a suitable alternative.

He watched her work, and finally she succeeded—a pipe came loose, but she grabbed it just before it fell to the stone floor. Bailey's heart beat faster as she cut off a handful of her hair with the stone and used the hair to tie the pipe back into place. Then she began scraping away at the next piece of electrical cord.

Bailey suddenly felt terrified. He knew the goblins would most likely keep him alive to trade for Henry, but what if they realized they didn't need Savannah alive at all?

Bailey pulled the ratatosker into the cage, tucking it inside his hoodie pocket, trying not to make any noise as it scrambled around tickling and scratching him. Finally, it curled into a ball and lay still.

One of the guards squinted and peered into Savannah's cage, becoming suspicious of her scraping. With her back to him, she couldn't see him coming closer. If Bailey didn't distract him, he would take away her stones and then they'd have no chance at all.

So Bailey did what he had to do. He totally flipped out.

"I need to get out of here! My head's gonna explode! I'm gonna pull my skin off! I can't take all this light anymore! Help me, help me! YOU HAVE TO LET ME OUT!"

"Shut up, boy. You can't go home to your daddy. You're our prisoner."

The goblins had no idea what would calm a human boy, so they patted his legs awkwardly. Savannah kept her back to them all, and he saw she was taking advantage of the opportunity. Her hand was moving faster, scraping the extension cord as fast as she could.

Bailey stood up and shook the bars of his prison. The pipes rattled and Bailey surprised himself with his own strength. Maybe, if he got angry enough, he could shake the bars apart with his bare hands.

"I need to get out! You have to let me out!"

The guards yelled at him to shut up as the other white-robed goblin guardians took notice and began surrounding their cages. Bailey knew Savannah didn't have much time. He had to convince all the goblins to focus on him.

"Listen to me, goblins," Bailey said earnestly. "Axel Pazuzu can't be trusted. No matter what he tells you, you have to understand that diving to the bottom of the ocean with Henry is impossible. That far out, the water is too deep for you. You can't trust him."

The goblins nearest him scoffed at the suggestion. "*You* can't be trusted, human," one of them spat back. "*You* destroy our cities with subways. *You* chop down the trees and replace them with concrete. *You* steal the stars and make them your slaves."

Capella stepped forward. She wore a white T-shirt robe like the others. "You humans are the ones that will do anything for money. You told me yourself that you agreed to put us in cages for seven thousand dollars."

All the other goblins gasped. Then one whispered, "Is seven thousand a lot of dollars?"

"It's a lot, I think," whispered another.

Canopus stamped his foot. "Irrelevant! A goblin's life is worth more than any amount of paper! And a star's life is worth more than any number of goblin lives. The giants *will* be grateful to us for returning their son and they *will* lift the stars back into the sky. Only a giant can lift a star so high."

"*Only a giant can lift a star so high,*" the goblins chanted together.

Bailey sighed. "You *must* listen. The sea giants, no matter how tall they are, cannot hang stars back in the sky. The stars haven't gone anywhere—they're still up there. You just can't see them because of all the light from our cities. It's called *ambient light*. We learned about it in earth science last year."

Canopus growled. "Lies, lies, all human lies!"

The other goblins picked up the chant. "LIES, LIES, ALL HUMAN LIES!"

Then Bailey thought of something.

"What if I could show you that the stars really are still hanging in the sky? What if I took one of you high up to see them? As high as a sea giant's head? Then you could see the stars are still there."

Canopus's eyes narrowed, as did all the other goblins'.

"Never trust a human," one whispered, and all of them bared their pointed yellow teeth.

Suddenly there was a clatter of pipes hitting the floor. Bailey turned, as did all the goblin guardians. Savannah had scraped the bindings of her cage floor completely away, allowing her to roll through the bottom and onto the sanctuary floor. Before a goblin could catch her, she ran to a reading lamp that glowed brightly against the cave wall. She grabbed it and held it high above her head with one hand. In her other hand she held a sharpened stone.

"STAND BACK, ALL OF YOU! Bailey Buckleby and I are leaving this place right now. *Or I will smash this star into smithereens.*"

All the goblins gasped in unison.

"I am *totally* serious," she said, threatening the lamp with her rock.

One of the guards snarled in contempt, but watching her carefully, he slowly unlocked Bailey's cage.

The other goblins took one step back and whispered, "Don't do it, girl. It's so fragile. *Please spare the star.*"

Savannah threatened the bulb with her rock. Bailey stepped out of his cage, and Canopus cracked his knuckles as if he was willing to make a different choice than his fellow goblins.

"Listen, Canopus," Bailey said quietly. "My offer stands. I have a friend who can fly us up to the sky, higher than the clouds. It will be dangerous, but once you're high enough, you'll be able to see all the stars. Wouldn't that be worth the risk? And wouldn't you love to deliver this good news to all of the Eighteenth Order? You could tell all goblins everywhere that the stars are alive and safe where they belong and you don't need to steal human lights anymore. The truth is up there. I promise you."

Canopus's green eyes glowed with hatred. "Why would I trust you? You and your father locked me in a cage."

"I'm not my father," Bailey said, and as soon as he said it, he realized this had always been true. Not all monsters were evil, and in fact, some of them deserved more respect than a lot of humans he knew. He had never needed Dr. March or even his mother to teach him this truth— only to confirm it.

Canopus took one step forward and Bailey took one step backward. The exit from the Starlight Sanctuary into the darkness of unknown tunnels lay just behind him.

"Bailey and I are leaving," Savannah insisted. "Give me my sword or this star gets it!"

Bailey wanted to make things right. "Canopus, let us go and I'll show you."

Canopus stared at them, grumbling as he considered Bailey's words. Finally, he turned and walked solemnly to a large plastic igloo chest that undoubtedly had been stolen from a human's garage. He flipped the latch and removed a beach towel bundle inside. He opened the towel to reveal Savannah's Bullhead sword and Bailey's single red Frisbee.

"And our phones," Savannah demanded, waving the rock at the lamp.

Canopus growled, cursing under his breath, but retrieved their phones from the chest. Bailey took them and inched slowly backward.

Canopus hissed and lifted his lip in contempt. "You speak as if you offer a choice, but there is none. If I don't let you leave, the girl destroys the star. If we can't ransom you for the baby sea giant, then the stars remain on the ground."

Bailey's shoes squished in mud as they walked backward out of the sanctuary. None of the goblins made a move.

"Come find me, Canopus," Bailey said earnestly. "I promise you that the Bucklebys will never hunt or harm a tunnel goblin again. And I also promise to prove to you that even if humans have destroyed goblin homes, they've left the stars in peace."

Canopus lifted his goggles to his forehead and blinked. Whether the goblin believed Bailey's promises or not, he couldn't know. The white-robed star protectors stared at them blankly as Bailey and Savannah took one more backward step into the yawning dark tunnel before turning to run.

CHAPTER TWENTY-FOUR

AARON AACKERMAN'S SIXTH-GRADE GRADUATION PARTY

BAILEY AND SAVANNAH soon found themselves alone in thick, muddy darkness with the Starlight Sanctuary only a faint glow behind them. Caverns loomed to the left and right and maybe even beneath them. They could barely tell because they could see only shadows against shadows.

Savannah waved her revolutionary sword in front of her to protect them from vengeful goblins or whatever else lived under the earth. Bailey stayed behind her so she didn't slice him. She should have been more afraid, Bailey thought. A certain amount of fear kept you sharp and from making foolish choices. Savannah showed none, and in fact, by the way she was swinging her blade, was almost longing for new foes.

"I have our way to get home, Savannah, but we'll need

light." Bailey scratched the back of the ratatosker in his hoodie pocket, keeping it calm and pressing it into a ball so it didn't dart away into the darkness. Bailey wanted so badly to set the little fuzzball down and let it direct them home, but without light, it would scurry away into the shadows, and their one chance to escape the muddy maze would be wasted.

"I wish I had grabbed a battery-powered star," Savannah joked, cutting the air with her sword, *zip, zip, zip*. "So, Bailey boy. Maybe this would be a good time to discuss your knowledge of underground monsters."

"I don't think you want to know," he said. Half of the monsters discussed in *In the Shadow of Monsters* resided underground, and they were the slimiest, creepiest half.

"Tell me," she whispered.

"Well, you know the Grand Canyon wasn't formed by a river. That's a myth. The canyon was formed by the movement of the giant snakes of Teotihuacan, which can grow over a thousand feet long. Their mouths can unhinge and swallow ten horses at a time. They travel underground and cause a lot of the earthquakes in California and Mexico. And it's not just goblins and the giant snakes of Teotihuacan that make tunnels—there are also the mole people, who are totally blind but will eat anything they smell, including humans—"

Finally, she showed fear. "You're right, Bailey boy. I don't want to know."

They walked without speaking for what seemed to be miles. They turned where the tunnels turned, they climbed uphill, they slid downhill, and one time they fell five feet from darkness into even deeper darkness. They had no idea if they were getting closer to the surface or going deeper or just going in circles.

They had no food. Worse, they had no water. Their phone batteries had died long ago, so they had no light or even a chance at reception. Savannah suggested they suck on the mud but Bailey didn't think they had reached that level of desperation just yet. He felt dizzy and slipped to his knees more and more frequently.

"Should we stop and sleep?" Savannah suggested.

"To be honest, I'm afraid I wouldn't wake up." He felt too weak to even cry and was glad, because despite how dire their circumstances had become, he still wanted so badly to be cool in front of this amazing girl and save the day.

Or save the night. He couldn't be sure which.

"Let's sit and rest for a minute," Savannah said. "I won't let you sleep. We'll sit for five minutes tops, then we'll make ourselves get up and keep moving."

They sat in the mud—Savannah right next to him, some part of her touching some part of him, but he could hardly even tell. "I'm cold," she said and snuggled into him, putting her head down on his because she was that much taller. He put his arm around her shoulder, trying not to be short.

"I promised you I wouldn't let you sleep."

"Then talk to me. Tell me how you got to be so tough."

There was a long pause in the dark. "Now you sound

like the girls in our class who make fun of me, like being tough is a bad thing."

Bailey wrapped his arm tighter around her. "I'm not making fun of you at all. I'm glad you're tough, Savannah. We're gonna need tough if we plan to escape these tunnels."

He felt her breath on his cheek. "My parents leave me home alone a lot. They go out to bars and come home late, so I've had to make myself be brave enough to face any monsters in the dark. I've always known they were out there and not just characters in stories, so I kept this sword under my bed, and even when I wasn't big enough to hold it, I liked knowing it was there. Reading stories about the Bullhead Brigade has always made me feel bigger and stronger. Sometimes I even pretend my great-great-great-great-grandfather's ghost watches over me."

Bailey felt her long, smooth hair between his fingers.

"I like that you don't call me Monster Boy," he said.

"I like that you showed me Abigail and Henry." After a long pause, she said, "It's so dark down here."

"I know," Bailey said. "Too dark."

For a while, they sat and said nothing. Bailey wondered if she had fallen asleep, but then she spoke up and startled him.

"Do you remember Aaron Aackerman's sixth-grade graduation party?"

"*Ugh*. Yes."

"Do you remember playing Seven Minutes in Heaven in Aaron's basement?"

Bailey did remember, unfortunately. With no parents

to interfere, the curious sixth graders of Whalefat Beach had decided to play a game that combined Spin the Bottle with Seven Minutes in Heaven. Ella Robertson didn't even want to play, but peer pressure and threats of exile from the basement to the Aackerman living room to watch *The Sound of Music* with Mrs. Aackerman and Aaron's five-year-old sister, Julie, drove Ella to the only alternative—to spin the bottle and sit in the dark in the basement closet with whomever the bottle chose.

And it chose Bailey.

The giggling sixth graders shut the closet door behind them, leaving the two alone with nothing but the darkness and the Aackermans' vacuum cleaner.

"I'm not kissing you," Ella Robertson said firmly somewhere in the black.

"No problem," Bailey had said.

"So stay on your side. Don't even let your feet touch me."

"Understood."

"I don't even like breathing the same air as you. I'll get your cooties," she hissed. "Everyone knows your family is cursed. My father says your father made a pact with the devil and that's why your mother is dead."

Bailey had said nothing, and they'd sat in silence. Had Ella been a boy, Bailey would have punched into the darkness, hoping to hit his face. But Ella was a girl, so he had to sit there for six and a half minutes with the insult hovering between them unanswered, while children outside egged them on with "*Oooooooh!*"

The memory made Bailey feel worse, but at least he hadn't fallen asleep.

"Well," Savannah said, "when it was my turn, you had already run up the stairs to watch *The Sound of Music*, I guess, because you left without saying a word to anybody. I had to spin the bottle and sit in the closet with Billy Dolby, who smelled like Cheetos and asked me if I wore a bra."

Bailey started laughing at the thought of that. "Okay, I thought my turn was bad, but you win, Savannah. That's a rough seven minutes."

"It was the longest, stupidest, cheesiest seven minutes of my life." She laughed. "Especially because I wanted to sit in the closet with you."

Silence. Then Bailey felt Savannah taking his hands in hers and locking their fingers together. He could feel the calluses that she had earned from many hours of Four-square and sword swinging. Holding her hands was so exciting, he thought he might faint. *But really*, he thought, *I'm just dying from dehydration.*

And then, as if the muddy tunnel around them wasn't dark enough, the world faded away to black and he was gone.

CHAPTER TWENTY-FIVE

TRY OR DIE

SAVANNAH'S FINGERS PULLED on Bailey's hoodie string, choking him and bringing him back to reality.

"I know how we can get out of here!" Savannah whispered suddenly, yanking the string free. "The ratatosker, of course! We can use this as a leash, and he can lead us back to your store."

Bailey considered her idea, floating in the dark. "I suppose we could tie it to his tusk. But it's not very long and ratatoskers go whatever direction is the fastest route— even if it's up or down a wall."

"We either try or die, Bailey boy." And he knew she was right.

Bailey held tight the ratatosker, whose little rat feet scrambled in the air like it had already been given a mission and was anxious to get going.

"Let's call him Snoopy," Savannah said, carefully tying the string to Snoopy's tusk with a double sailor knot.

"Why Snoopy?" Bailey asked, his throat parched.

"Because he's going to be our beagle to find our way home. Also, I like *Peanuts*."

After checking the string to make sure it was tight enough, Bailey set Snoopy down on the mud floor of the tunnel and let him sniff the fragment of his father's pizza-stained sweatshirt. Snoopy sniffed the cloth, then stood up on his hind legs to sniff the air, did an about-face, and led them back the way they had come.

"Backward?" Savannah asked.

"We have to trust him," Bailey said, feeling like he might faint.

Snoopy pulled hard against the string, so Bailey wrapped it once around his wrist. They walked in silence for a long time, turning when Snoopy wanted to turn. When the ratatosker jumped down, they jumped after him, but when Snoopy tried to scramble up the mud wall of the tunnel, they faced a problem.

"How are we supposed to get up there?" Savannah asked. He bent down and she climbed onto his shoulders. "*Yes*! There is a tunnel going straight up here, but I don't feel much to grab on to."

"Get down, Savannah. We can't risk it. Even if we could climb up, we can't see anything, and it would be too easy to reach out for nothing and fall to our death."

Bailey sat down while Snoopy jumped up and down like a bouncing ball, anxious to lead the way.

"How can we get him to show us another route? There's got to be another way out of here."

"We have to walk in another direction for a while and then eventually he will find another way to the store—like GPS when you go off course and it reroutes itself to your destination."

"Excellent. Let's go."

Despite Snoopy's protests, they walked determinedly up a slope for what seemed to be hours, turning whenever they ran into a wall. After they thought they had gone far enough, Bailey put down Snoopy, who immediately tried to pull them down another damp slope.

"Can we sit here for a moment?" Bailey asked. He was dizzier than she was, and even though they were in complete darkness, he was seeing red and yellow spots.

"Okay," Savannah said. Bailey felt her body next to him, exuding warmth. She pulled a clump of mud from the wall and put it in her mouth.

"What are you doing?"

She spit it out. "Gross. I thought I might suck some water out of the mud. But that *definitely* doesn't work."

"I would do anything for some goblin pool water now," Bailey said. "We should have taken some."

"I know. I wish I had thought of that. I just wanted to get us out of there."

"You *did* get us out of there, Savannah. You're amazing.

You're not scared of anything. I'm glad you're here with me. Anyone else would have given up and we'd still be in cages. You're made for monster hunting."

"Well, then, maybe you can hire me at Buckleby and Son's. I need a part-time job. I hate babysitting because toddlers drool all over everything."

"You're hired," Bailey said, making an executive decision.

"Thanks, boss," she whispered.

Bailey rested his head against the tunnel wall. Strangely, it seemed to be vibrating. "Do you feel that?" he said as softly as he could. He stood up, holding his breath so he could hear better. Snoopy bounced up and down and squeaked.

"Hush, Snoopy, I'm trying to hear," Savannah whispered, and Bailey picked up Snoopy with both hands and brought him close to his chest to keep him quiet, because now they both felt and heard something.

Something rolling.

It sounded like a tire rolling through mud that with each rotation made a *slurp, slurp, slurp*, and it was approaching quickly.

"Oh no," Bailey said when he realized what it was. "Run!"

"Which way?"

"Any way!"

The rolling and slurping grew louder, and they immediately realized which way *not* to run. The sound was coming right toward them.

"Bailey? What is it?"

"I think it smells the ratatosker," Bailey whispered. "Or *us*."

"What does?"

The rumbling grew louder. It was approaching at terrific speed.

"We can't outrun it. Plaster yourself against the wall."

They both flattened themselves against the tunnel wall with their backs pressed into the mud. "Bailey," she whispered in his ear. "*Tell me what's going on.*"

The thing slurped very close to them now.

"Remember the hoop snakes I showed you in the shop?"

"Yeah?"

"The scientific name for them is *Serpens interminus minisculus*."

"Okay . . ."

"Well, some hoop snakes aren't so minisculus."

In fact, the hoop snake that rolled past them was *Serpens interminus magnum*. They felt its scales brush their noses as it rolled by, and soon it rolled to a muddy stop. Then nothing. Then the slurping turned and started coming back toward them again.

"It won't miss next time!" Bailey croaked, his throat dry from dehydration and fear. "Run!"

They ran but felt it gaining on them as it rolled over and over, making the hideous *slurp, slurp, slurp* sound as it wheeled through the mud, coming closer and closer.

Bailey decided it was pointless for them both to die. The snake might be satisfied eating just one of them, and he might as well fight before being digested. "Savannah, give me your sword. I'll face it head-on."

He heard her slice it through the darkness.

"We both will," she whispered. Standing in front of Bailey, she took both hands and lifted the sword so that the giant hoop snake would wheel right on top of them and stab itself, hopefully in a vital organ. Bailey hated to kill anything, but he could see no other option if they were to survive.

Snoopy struggled in his grip, trying to get out of his hands.

"Get ready," Savannah said as the rumbling, turning, wheeling beast was nearly upon them. All they could see were its eyes, like two pinpoints of yellow in the distant dark. Then the beast rolled again and its eyes were bigger and brighter, like headlights approaching. One more roll and they could see huge yellow eyes with red slits down the middles, the glow from them illuminating its entire head. They could see the details of it now, its great un-hinged jaw holding its own tail firmly as the eyes focused on them, turning for one final roll.

"This is it," Savannah said, holding the blade tight

and strong because they both knew they would only get one chance to drive it into the snake's flesh.

But Snoopy pulled hard against his string leash. He wanted to jump out of Bailey's arms and go left. Bailey had just a second to make a decision, to stay put with the blade or to follow Snoopy. He pulled on Savannah as hard as he could and left their fates up to the little ratatosker.

They fell down a slide of mud that grew wetter and wetter as they tumbled. Bailey felt his mouth filling with mud as the walls of the tunnel closed in on them. Behind them, they heard the snake slithering toward them as it unwound itself to travel by conventional serpentine means. Bailey looked back once. The yellow eyes with red slits had not lost their focus.

They crawled on as the tunnel tightened around them. He thought at any moment they would hit a dead end of mud and then they would become the giant creature's lunch. Bailey had fed so many live mice to the hoop snakes in their cage. Strange that his life would end like this—to feed a hoop snake one last time.

Then his head bumped into wood.

Savannah politely knocked.

"There's a door here. *With a knob*."

"Well, hurry up and open it!" Bailey yelled, because he understood now what adults meant when they said they were claustrophobic. He felt sick, squeezed into a hole with barely enough room to crawl. They could hear the snake writhing through the narrow tunnel toward them. It was so close, its glowing yellow eyes illuminated the door in the darkness.

Savannah turned the knob and pulled the door open. A smaller tunnel loomed before them. She crawled into it and Bailey followed. He shut the door behind them and they heard the snake thump into it.

"I hope this leads somewhere," Bailey said, "because that snake won't be stopped for long."

"There's a rope here," Savannah said excitedly, and she must have pulled it, because suddenly Bailey wasn't thirsty anymore. Water engulfed them in the darkness.

He couldn't see or hear or breathe. He flailed his arms around, and Snoopy swam free. He tried to kick upward, but he couldn't even be sure which way was up.

Then something grabbed him and lifted him up toward the light.

Light. He was so happy to see light again. Even if he was drowning, he was grateful—anything was better than dying in unknown darkness.

They all broke the surface: Bailey, Savannah, Snoopy, and the minotaur maze-maker from the Mojave Desert— Nikos Tekton.

CHAPTER TWENTY-SIX

GREED HAS DRIVEN THE DEMON TO MADNESS

"**ARE YOU KIDS** still alive? Spit the water out, because we must start moving."

The minotaur dragged them to the edge of the water by their wet and muddy shirts like half-drowned cats. Bailey and Savannah sat up and spit out water, mud, and weeds.

"I know you have undergone quite a harrowing experience, children, but time is of the essence."

Bailey felt his right hand being jerked away from him. Snoopy's leash had tangled between his fingers, and the bedraggled ratatosker was determinedly pulling, trying to lead them out of the water.

"I know where we are," Bailey said as reality began to settle into place around him. "We're at Mr. Hanson's pond."

"Yes," Nikos said. "This pond is one of the entrances to the goblin tunnels. This little girl led me to it."

Nikos pulled another ratatosker from the pocket of his work pants. Bailey recognized her as one of theirs, with white eyebrows, white whiskers, and exceptionally long tusks.

"So you got into our store and stole her?"

"Not at all," Nikos said. "Your father gave her to me. Candycane refused to pay me, so your father and I came to a suitable arrangement—I agreed to help find you. I must admit, I prefer to take employment with your father than Candycane—he's a far more honorable man."

While the female ratatosker sat perfectly still and content—her mission to find Bailey and Savannah complete—Snoopy pulled hard against the wet leash, still determined to reach Bailey's father.

"Hey, Snoopy, home is that way," Bailey said, pointing in the opposite direction.

"Yes," Nikos said, returning the female ratatosker to one pants pocket and removing his Jeep keys from the other. "But your father isn't at your store. He is rapidly approaching Whalefat Marina. We must catch up to him. Please, children, we must go. He's not answering his phone, and I fear the worst. We must get to him before he tries something crazy."

Nikos helped Savannah up. Bailey saw John Hanson peeking from his living room window, very alarmed by what he was seeing. He was pale and quivering, and Bailey wondered why such a man would choose to live in a town like Whalefat Beach, known for monster troubles and worse—tourists.

Bailey checked his phone, but the battery remained dead. "I'm not sure we should trust you. You could still be working for Mr. Boom. Just tell me why my father is on his way to the marina, and Savannah and I will make our own decisions."

Nikos dropped to one knee to look Bailey in the eye. His big bull mouth frowned with pity. "Your father thinks you've been captured by Axel Pazuzu. He's agreed to give Axel the baby sea giant in exchange for you and Savannah. Your father loves you dearly. Please let me earn your trust, Bailey Buckleby. I know what the cynocephaly really intends to do, and it is frightening. Greed has driven the demon to madness. You defeated me honorably with courage and cleverness, and now I am proud to be in your family's service. If you will trust me for just a little while, I'll explain in the Jeep."

CHAPTER TWENTY-SEVEN

IN DANGER ONCE AGAIN

SEVERAL DRIVERS in the opposite lane swerved their cars into the ditch when they saw a seven-foot-tall minotaur driving a Jeep down Highway 1 toward Whalefat Marina with the top down. The September sky had grown dark and gray, even during the daytime, and wind and rain seemed inevitable. Bailey looked up to see six black helicopters flying overhead toward the Farallon Islands, far to the west.

Nikos, whose giant hands practically engulfed the steering wheel as he drove, kept looking from the road to the sky. "The wind demon is making his move. Those are military helicopters."

"Is that dog-head creating this storm?" Savannah asked, unable to resist playing with the two ratatoskers in the cage in the backseat.

"Indirectly," Nikos said. "He speaks the language of the sea giants and is quite adept at lying. He's told the sea giants he is going to give them back their son, although he has no intention of doing so." Nikos turned the Jeep radio to the news as they curved along the cliffs rising above the beaches.

"Northern Californians are advised to evacuate their homes and drive inland. The expected earthquake and floods are predicted to be far worse than those that destroyed San Francisco seven years ago. The Coast Guard has issued a warning to all vessels to go ashore. Abandon your boats and drive inland. Repeat—all citizens are to drive inland immediately. Californian lives are in danger once again."

"The ancient sea giants are rising. They seek their lost son, and they won't give up this time."

Bailey already feared what Axel Pazuzu could do with Henry. "If the sea giants destroyed San Francisco when they were looking for their lost baby before—"

"Oh no," Savannah said, realizing the horror. "That dog-head could bring Henry to any city on the coast he wanted and destroy it, too!"

"Which he will threaten to do," Nikos said, "unless he is paid. It has been his plan to hold all the world to ransom, starting with Los Angeles for three billion in gold."

"Three billion in gold?" Savannah exclaimed. "That's crazy!"

"The cynocephaly has convinced himself the city will pay it."

"My dad *can't* give him Henry," Bailey said desperately, but he already knew his father would if he thought that's what it would take to save him. He plugged his phone into the Jeep's cigarette lighter to call his father, but there was no answer.

Nikos pressed the gas and turned onto Marina Way. The Golden Gate Bridge, an enormous mangled ball of red metal, took center stage of the dramatic skyline of stormy skies—a reminder of the horrible damage two desperate sea giants could leave in the wake of their grief. Lightning flashed against the western sky. For just a second, Bailey saw what used to be the Farallon Islands silhouetted against the sky. Now the islands were rising, forming the shapes of heads and shoulders.

Bailey looked at the single red Frisbee in his lap.

"We need to make a stop. I need to buy more ammo," he said.

"There isn't much time," Nikos said.

"There's a sporting goods store up ahead on the right. Pull over."

There was only traffic heading north as they hurried south. Against his better judgment, Nikos whipped the Jeep over and into the store's parking lot. Bailey put his hand out.

"I need a hundred dollars."

"What? Young Buckleby, I'm in dire financial straits. I have too much debt for a minotaur my age. One hundred dollars is a great sum for me!"

"Mr. Tekton," Savannah said with her most serious

voice, squeezing in between the front seats of the Jeep, "I have two things to show you. The first thing is this sword."

Nikos turned around, and when he saw the hilt of the sword bearing the silver bullhead, his big eyes began to well with tears.

"Where did you get that sword, young lady?"

"My great-great-great-great-grandfather gave it to me. He was a captain in the Bullhead Brigade."

"The Bullhead Brigade," Nikos said quietly, in awe. "May I hold it?"

Savannah handed the sword to him in both palms. Bailey tried his best to be patient.

Nikos held up the sword so he could examine the bullhead carving on the hilt and the intricacy of the designs etched into the blade. "This sword was crafted at a time when men fought side by side with minotaurs for the freedom to rule their lands as they wished. They fought like warriors against the British to protect their farms and their mazes." Nikos caressed the weapon with his big bull hands, letting the sharp blade cut his flesh slightly. A single bead of his red blood trickled down its edge. "Those were different times," he said sadly. "Savannah Mistivich, I am honored to know you."

Savannah smiled and reached into her hoodie pocket. "Bullheads should help each other. I collected this from the ceiling of the goblin tunnels." She opened her hands to reveal a pile of small gold nuggets, all sparkling in the storm-infected sunlight. "If you help us, Mr. Tekton, all this gold is yours. It should help you pay off your debt."

His bull eyes widening, the minotaur quickly calculated the value of what she held in her hands. He reached into his pocket and handed all the bills he had to Bailey, who then ran into the store.

"You honor me, young lady, with an honor I have yet to earn."

Savannah put her arms around his thick bull neck and hugged him hard. "Take this," she said, and she poured the gold chunks into Nikos's hands. He choked on the thank-you he tried to deliver, because after so many months of humiliating debt, he had lost his faith in everybody and—worst of all—himself.

A few minutes later, Bailey was running across the parking lot toward them with twenty Frisbees, ten under each arm. He jumped into the Jeep.

"Hurry," he said as calmly as he could, because the sudden realization that he could lose not one parent but two was rapidly filling him with an emptiness that he feared would make him more hole than human.

But he was a Buckleby and a Whalefatian. He had to be strong. He had to be the vanguard. Axel Pazuzu had to be stopped. His father and millions of human lives were depending on him, as well as three sea giants. As Nikos drove, Bailey unwrapped the Frisbees from their plastic packaging. He knew he had all a man needed—twenty-one Frisbees, his wits, and a determination to fight for what was right—even if it cost him his own life.

CHAPTER TWENTY-EIGHT

PUNKS

THE HIGHWAY EXIT to Whalefat Marina was barricaded by military trucks and Humvees, but Nikos knew another way.

"Hold on to your horns, we're going off-roading."

Savannah grabbed the back of Nikos's seat with both hands and screamed, "We don't have horns!" The minotaur turned the Jeep off the highway and down a green slope of the Marin headlands at a very steep angle.

"Don't roll us!" Bailey wailed.

"Trust me, young Buckleby."

The Jeep caught air more than once as it bounced down the grassy hill toward the marina access road below. Nikos veered between several eucalyptus trees, increasing speed as he did. Bailey wondered if the minotaur had done this before—he seemed to almost be enjoying it.

Ahead of them, Bailey saw two slabs of slate sticking up out of the ground. Nikos gripped the steering wheel hard as if he had already made his decision.

"No," Bailey screamed.

"We must," Nikos declared victoriously.

"What?" Savannah yelled. But two seconds later she realized the minotaur's intentions as Nikos hit the gas and the Jeep wheels made contact with the rock. The seven-foot-tall Labyrinthian pulled on the steering wheel and leaned back as far as he could.

And they were airborne.

"We're flying!" Savannah screamed with excitement because she had never been in an airplane before, let alone a flying Jeep. Their front end pointed up to the sky, and after what seemed whole minutes, the rear wheels of the Jeep touched grass and Bailey flew up into the air before landing again in his seat. He quickly put on his seat belt.

Nikos laughed and swerved the Jeep through the grass and onto the access road, nearly running over the snow-cone guy on his tricycle, who was desperately pedaling up the hill to get away from whatever danger lay below at the marina. Thunder cracked above them, and just as their Jeep swerved into the opposite lane, the snow-cone guy yelled, "PUNKS!"

Bailey and Savannah did not need to ask what he was pedaling away from. Ahead of them, giant waves splashed against the docks, and boats bobbed high in the water. The surfers showed no fear, running out to catch the most tubular waves of the year. And way out on the horizon, the sea giants could be seen taking great steps in slow motion, their elbows above the water now, dark gray storm clouds obscuring their faces.

Hysterical tourists, who had only come to Whalefat Marina for a pleasant diversion, were now running to their cars in the parking lot in pure panic. No matter whether they thought the giants they saw rising from the ocean were real or not, their reaction was the same—*run*.

Nikos Tekton scanned the crowd of crazed vacationers.

"He's here. Somewhere."

Bailey saw them first. "There." He pointed.

They were standing on the docks next to a slick motor yacht painted in alternating red and white stripes. On the bow of the boat, the name was written in bold letters—*The Sweet Tooth*. Candycane Boom wore his puffy black coat to protect himself from the wind. The four slouching sophomores turned to watch Nikos swerve the Jeep right onto the dock. Bailey leapt out over the Jeep door, because he had always wanted to do that. He readied a Frisbee in each hand.

"Do I need to teach you juvenile delinquents another lesson?" Bailey yelled against the wind and the roar of the ocean.

The sophomores snarled and prepared to pounce, but Mr. Boom smacked Fuzzy in the head with the back of his hand.

"At ease, dum-dums."

Nikos and Savannah stepped out to flank Bailey.

Savannah waved her sword in front of her like she meant to use it. The tenth graders stepped back like beaten wet rats.

"No need for a fight," Mr. Boom said. "The real villain has just left the scene, and he didn't pay me, either. If I get the chance, I'm going to snap his dog-neck in half."

"What goes around comes around," Nikos said flatly, his bull nostrils flaring. "He didn't pay you, and *you* didn't pay *me*."

"Bouncing Betty, Nikos! How could I pay *you* if the demon didn't pay *me*? He was supposed to pay me one hundred and fifty thousand if I delivered Henry to him."

Bailey looked up into Mr. Boom's big-framed eyes. "Did you give him Henry?" he demanded, trying to keep calm and focused, though he badly wanted to hurt this man.

"I did not," he said with his bottom lip turned up. "I merely suggested to the dog-head that if anything would motivate your father to leave the Buckleby fortress it would be a threat to his son. When the goblins carried you and your girlfriend off, I thought Pazuzu had successfully captured you. But he said you were not in his possession and he therefore could not make any idle threat. I reminded him that your father didn't know that, so the demon dressed up two pillows in hoodies to look like you both. He put them on his boat, far enough out to sea so that your father wouldn't be able to recognize you without binoculars. In his haste, your father did not bring binoculars, and so thought that you and this young lady were the wind demon's captives."

"Where are they now?" Savannah asked in panic.

Candycane handed Bailey his binoculars and pointed out to sea. Through them Bailey could see a Bermuda rigged sloop with two tall brilliant yellow sails jigging and jagging toward the giant torsos haloed by lightning flashes. The sloop was towing two aluminum fishing boats—the first piled high with desk lamps, Christmas tree lights, headlamps, chandeliers, and streetlights, while the second boat contained twelve small figures seated in three rows of four.

"Your father and Henry are on that sailboat—*with him.*"

"We need to get to him," Bailey said urgently.

"I wouldn't, boy," Mr. Boom said. "The wind demon has your father and Henry tied up and is delivering them to certain doom. Even if you could reach them before they get to the giants, a great storm is coming, and that demon can make things worse. He has my megaphone."

"So what if he has a megaphone?" Savannah said, her sword pointed at his nose.

"A cynocephaly's lies are deadlier than most," Nikos said gravely. "With a megaphone, the giants will be able to hear his lies, and in their desperation to find their son, they will be likely to believe him."

"The minotaur speaks the truth," Mr. Boom said. "If

I were you, Bailey, I would weigh my odds and make the sensible decision—give your father up to his fate and sell your shop to me. Take the profit and invest in yourself. Go to college. Get yourself a degree in software programming. Give yourself the best gift a smart boy can give himself—a comfortable future. Your father has lost his wife and now himself. You deserve better, son. Go home."

Bailey felt anger bubbling inside him. The desire for revenge filled him, and he knew that if he said only one word, Nikos would throw punches and Savannah would swing her sword, and Candycane Boom would be on the dock bleeding to death. But instead of responding violently to his insults—which was so tempting—he calculated the exact number that would motivate his opponent.

"How much to rent your yacht?"

The four sophomores snickered. Mr. Boom stomped on Chinless's foot, and the scrawny boy squealed like a poked pig.

"Bailey, you're my favorite young adult, but you can't afford to rent *The Sweet Tooth*, especially since I know you intend to drive it to its inevitable destruction, as well as your own. I can't have your blood on my hands. Also, I really do love this boat."

Lightning cracked. Behind him, Bailey heard sirens approaching and scared citizens screaming. The wind was whipping against them and even the earth was beginning to shake. The giants' heads loomed high up in the clouds, their arms slowly swinging like deadly pendulums, and

Axel Pazuzu was getting away, taking his father and Henry with him.

Bailey took a long breath as he considered the right price.

"Seventy-five thousand dollars. If you drive this yacht for us for one day, I will get my father back and pay you seventy-five thousand in cash, even if it takes the rest of my life to do so."

Mr. Boom laughed deeply from his evil belly. "Bailey! My life is worth far more than that! To risk my own life for your father's is beyond negotiation, and besides, I know you can never earn that much in my lifetime. The monster business isn't that lucrative, even for a smart little man like yourself."

"Ninety thousand," Bailey said evenly. Savannah gasped.

Mr. Boom stopped laughing. Bailey, skilled negotiator, knew he had him within the realm of possibility. "Young man, listen. I've always liked you. But—"

"One hundred thousand!" Savannah piped up in all seriousness. "And the debt will be mine as well as Bailey's."

Bailey saw a look of determination on Savannah's face that he had already grown to love, but still he said, "Savannah, really. This will have to be my debt and mine alone."

Nikos stepped forward, towering over all of them. If he wanted, he could put Boom's bald head between his giant hands and crush it like a watermelon. Instead, Nikos pressed the pile of gold nuggets Savannah had given him into the loan shark's chest.

"Here is a down payment for the children's cause."

Mr. Boom's eyebrows rose nearly off the top of his big bald head. He scraped at one of the nuggets with his thumbnail and whistled with greed. "Are you sure, friend? This looks like enough gold to pay off a certain minotaur's debt."

The minotaur bowed his head. "The boy and girl need this gold more than me. A man's life and a baby sea giant's reunion with his parents depend on it. It is my honor, or at least, my attempt to regain it."

Mr. Boom weighed the gold in his hand. "Won't you keep Henry for yourself, son?"

"No," Bailey said sadly. "I'll give him back to his parents." And as soon as he said it, he felt a swelling pride knowing that his father was right after all—Bailey was his mother's son with a heart big enough to prove it.

"One hundred and twenty thousand," Mr. Boom said quickly.

"Mr. Tekton," Bailey said. "Hit him."

The minotaur cocked his right arm back.

"Okay!" Mr. Boom said. "Fine, you little schemer! One hundred thousand, then. But you only get *The Sweet Tooth* until midnight. And that is my last offer. Suffering Sally, I won't even get to spend it because you're determined to kill us all!"

"Deal," Bailey said, and he shook the thug's hand, even though Candycane Boom had threatened bloody and painful torture upon him just days before. Business was business, and Axel Pazuzu was now far out to sea.

"I assume you want to leave right now?" Mr. Boom asked.

Bailey nodded and they climbed aboard.

CHAPTER TWENTY-NINE

THE SWEET TOOTH

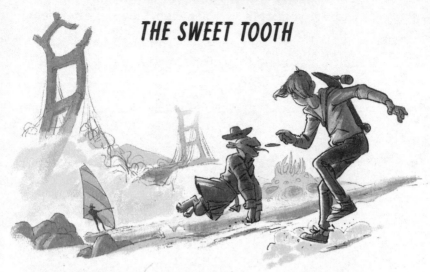

ABIGAIL WAS in the cabin below. Her tall brass cage had been jammed in between the leather pullout bench and the wet bar. She looked quite perturbed in her new quarters, and when she saw Bailey and Savannah, she let them know just how she felt with a *chirp, chirp* and a *CHIRP!*

Bailey shot Candycane a look of disgust. "You took Abigail. Why would you do that?"

Mr. Boom had to lower his head to enter the cabin. He sat down on the bench and locked his fingers together.

"I wouldn't concern yourself with Abigail. You've got a much bigger problem, namely that our contract doesn't include me fighting a wind demon for you. You have to do that all by yourself, and that's *if* we can catch up to him. So we shouldn't waste any more time discussing who took who."

Bailey had one of his newly purchased Frisbees in his right hand. With a quick flick of the wrist, he chopped it down on Candycane Boom's left knee.

"Dancing Dolly, that smarts!" It had been so many years since anyone had even considered physically assaulting him that he had forgotten how to defend himself or even how to react. He fell to the cabin floor, gripping his knee.

"You really should respect your elders, kid!"

"You took Abigail—an innocent, sweet harpy who had no part in any of this."

"Well, when your father surrendered himself to Axel Pazuzu along with Henry, he asked me to take care of her."

Bailey had grown adept at identifying lies lately. He whacked the Frisbee sideways into the thug's left ear.

"Cussing Catherine, stop it!"

"My father has never given a monster to anyone for free, let alone the man who just tried to kill us. You took her when you saw the chance. After we save my father and Henry, you *will* return her."

It had been so many years since anyone had even considered giving Mr. Boom a direct order, he had forgotten how to reply. So as his ear began to swell into a red beet, he merely grunted, "Okay."

Abigail whistled, *chiiiiirp!*

Bailey started to formulate a plan. "This yacht should be faster than a sailboat, right?"

Mr. Boom groaned as he sat up, holding his ear. "*The*

Sweet Tooth is a Riviera 4400. I can get this baby up to thirty knots."

"Is that fast enough to catch up to the dog-head?" Savannah asked as they followed him up to the deck.

"It's as fast as this yacht can go." He shrugged. "You get what you pay for. Success in your mission was not part of our contract."

Bailey saw the cynocephaly's yellow sails on the horizon, and even farther away, what looked like twin mountains on the move. The sea giants were creating waves that already rocked *The Sweet Tooth* from side to side and threatened to tip it over. Above them, Bailey saw the underbellies of helicopters charging forward.

Bailey took command. "Drive."

CHAPTER THIRTY

BETRAYED

IS IT EMBARRASSING for a heroic monster hunter who grew up on the shore of the Pacific Ocean to get seasick? Bailey wished he could steel his belly, especially when Savannah was running up and down the deck of the little yacht with ease, even as it bobbed up and down on the choppy waves. But instead, he leaned over the aft side of *The Sweet Tooth* and puked his guts out. Dehydration and lack of sleep and the fear that he might not save his father and Henry in time did not help matters, but luckily Savannah was not the sort of prude to be grossed out by a bit of vomit. In fact, she found a towel in the galley and wiped it off his face.

With the swells caused by the oncoming sea giants' footsteps, the yacht bobbed up ten feet and often caught air before it dropped back down. The wind from the storm pushed back at them, too, and several times Mr. Boom shouted from the steering wheel that they ought to turn back before the boat flipped. He yelled that they would surely drown.

"What good will one hundred grand do me if I'm dead?" he screamed into the wind, but Nikos stood in front of him, fists clenched, threatening his former employer with a different kind of painful death if he tried to turn the yacht back to shore.

Candycane Boom was, from bald head to big toe, an entirely selfish thug. But somewhere under his puffy winter coat burned a small ember of compassion. He removed a package of Dramamine from his pocket and handed it to the minotaur.

"Give this to the boy. He's going to need all his strength."

Nikos gave the tablets to Bailey, who swallowed them whole.

"When we overtake the wind demon's sailboat, we must be ready to fight," Nikos said, placing his giant fingers gently on Bailey's shoulder. "The sea giants will do *anything* to have their son returned to them, and knowing this, Axel will use their son like a carrot on a stick—baiting them—keeping them under his command. He'll lead them to Los Angeles, tell them their son is there, and then lead them on with more and more lies. He intends to threaten every coastal human city with destruction if he isn't paid in gold."

"He could blackmail humans forever," Bailey said,

shaking his head, willing himself to stop retching. "Why does he want gold so badly?"

Nikos shrugged. "Like all cynocephali, he's addicted to getting gold and addicted to losing it. In the past, he's invested in a hot-air balloon mail delivery service for non-humans, holiday sweaters for cats and dogs, and even iceberg vacation homes for yeti, but they were all very poor investments. You'd think after a few thousand years on this planet, wind demons would have a better grasp of consumer trends."

Axel Pazuzu's sloop was zigzagging into the wind ahead of them, tugging along the two rowboats. *The Sweet Tooth* was indeed gaining on them, having the advantage of a motor and no weighted rowboats tethered behind it.

In twenty minutes, Bailey felt his stomach calming, but the waves only grew, throwing *The Sweet Tooth* up and down like a rubber ducky in a baby's tub. Thankfully, the Dramamine kicked in, and Bailey gripped a Frisbee between both hands with determination.

Savannah raised her sword above her head.

"We will fight him together," she said as Candycane kept the pedal down and the distance between the boats began to visibly shorten.

Nikos smiled broadly at Savannah. "I will be honored to fight alongside a descendant of the Bullhead Brigade. When humans have an honorable cause to fight for, they rise to become their best selves. The Bullhead Brigade fought for freedom, and we fight for the innocent who know not what threatens them. You know, young lady, you

207

might really have minotaur blood running in your veins. Our species have intermingled once or twice."

"Really?" Savannah said, proud as could be. "No wonder I'm so strong!"

Candycane yelled over the roar of the waves and the wind. "What the blazes do you nuts want me to do? Ram her? Give me a plan, kid!"

And then they saw him.

Axel appeared on the bow of his boat and stood looking at them through a pair of binoculars. He wore the same slick black wet suit that he was wearing when Bailey met him on the shore of Whalefat Beach days ago. Then he lowered the binoculars and gave them all a friendly wave.

The twelve goblins in scuba gear stood up, not much taller than the sides of the rowboats that had been buffeted by the waves so much that they had become quite waterlogged. It was their weight that had been keeping the sloop from reaching its maximum speed, allowing *The Sweet Tooth* to come so close. The wind demon had proven that he could deftly maneuver a sailboat, but even he could not outrace a Riviera 4400 if he was weighed down by a boatload of goblins and a pile of electrical lighting fixtures.

Which is why Axel knelt down at the bow end of the boat and began to unloosen the knots.

"What is he doing?" Savannah gasped in horror.

"*No*," Bailey said desperately. "He can't do that to them."

"They will drown!" Nikos shouted over the wind,

looking over the side as *The Sweet Tooth* quickly gained on the drifting rowboats.

"Let them drown!" Mr. Boom yelled from the steering wheel, swerving to avoid crashing into the abandoned rowboat full of lighting fixtures.

"No, we can't!" Savannah shouted back.

The goblins in the drifting rowboat stood up and begged for Axel to come back, but not for very long. Once they saw their rowboat of fallen stars thrown about on the surface of the turbulent ocean, they all took up oars and started paddling heroically toward it. Bailey watched as the boat full of lights bounced off a wave and came crashing down. A chandelier fell into the water.

One brave goblin jumped in after it.

"Quick," Bailey said. "We have to get that boat and get the lights up in here, otherwise all those goblins will go in after them." He watched as the goblin swam toward the chandelier as it bobbed and began to sink. The goblin dove under the water and grabbed it in time, and the other goblins in scuba gear cheered and applauded her victory.

"Are you crazy?" Candycane yelled over his shoulder. Savannah was tying a nylon rope to the deck with a tight slip knot.

"Let's go," she said, ready to dive into the water.

"No," Nikos said. "You children will freeze to death. We're in the middle of the Pacific Ocean. This water is too cold!"

Bailey gripped the handrail. "I promised the goblins a Buckleby would never harm them again. Letting them drown is the same thing." He ran up to Mr. Boom. "Go alongside the boat carrying the lights," he said urgently.

"Okay, kid. It's your dime."

Candycane tried to steer alongside the rowboat, but it was obvious to Bailey that Axel's sloop was rapidly getting away.

Bailey stood up on the rails. "I'm going to jump." The goblins in the other boat were all standing up now, most of them anxiously covering their mouths with their hands.

Savannah tied the rope to his waist. She kissed him on the cheek and whispered in his ear, *"You can do it, Bailey boy."*

Without hesitation, he jumped—and landed on a stack of headlights. The goblins gasped, horrified that his fall might have broken one, but all the lights remained intact. Bailey tied the rope to the rowboat and Nikos started pulling him in.

"I'm next!" Savannah yelled, already tying another rope to her waist.

"No, girl, don't!" Nikos protested, reaching out to stop her before she jumped. But she leapt—into the goblins' rowboat. She fell short because their driver hadn't even been given time to get close enough. But the goblins pulled her out of the water and patted her on the back for her bravery. She tethered the rowboats to each other and to *The Sweet Tooth* so that they had both rowboats in tow. Candycane brought the yacht to a stop as they hoisted up Bailey, Savannah, all twelve goblins, and every last one of the electrical lights.

"Are you really going to let those wild animals ride with us?" he asked.

While the other goblins checked on their fallen stars to make sure none had broken, Capella spoke up. "We have no intention of eating you, sir. We appreciate the effort you have made. We obviously have been betrayed."

"Obviously," Canopus said mournfully.

Capella bowed her head in shame. Canopus put his arm around her. "It's okay," he said. "At least we didn't lose the stars."

"Or our gold," Capella muttered.

"Gold?" Candycane asked, his eyes widening as his suspicion of the goblins was immediately replaced with ravenous greed.

"The gold we were going to pay Mr. Pazuzu," she said, showing them seven T-shirts tied into bundles that each contained hundreds of tiny gold nuggets. "These bundles are heavy and helped keep the boat from flipping over. He was going to translate for us. We were going to dive into the sea and give the giants their son, and Mr. Pazuzu was going to politely ask them in their language if they could repay the favor by putting the stars back in the sky. That's all we wanted from him—just to ask a simple question. Why would he cut us loose?"

Nikos couldn't help but pull at his own beard at the sight of so much gold. "Cynocephali always choose the wrong investment, my little friend. Clearly he should have invested in you."

CHAPTER THIRTY-ONE

HIT THE GAS

MR. BOOM WANTED to start counting the gold nuggets, but Bailey reminded him that he had been hired for one job only—to drive *The Sweet Tooth* until midnight.

"Hit the gas!" Bailey commanded, and they were chasing Axel Pazuzu again. *We must reach him before he gets to the giants*, Bailey thought. *Before he can feed them his lies.*

He saw the sloop's yellow sails turn dramatically, cutting through the wind and sending the boat directly south. Mr. Boom wasted no time, pulling hard on the wheel as he angled toward the escaping craft.

"What's that dog-head doing?" Savannah yelled, the ocean wind soaking and whipping her hair back as she stepped up onto the rail to get a closer look. The cynocephaly stood at the stern of his boat staring straight at them.

"His plans are wicked and cruel," Capella said to Bailey. "We should never have trusted such a horrible creature."

Thunder cracked, and a second formation of helicopters flew over their heads.

Axel lifted his megaphone up to his dog lips. "STOP FOLLOWING ME! IT'S VERY RUDE!"

"You're rude!" Savannah shouted as loudly as her lungs would allow, but the wind blew her retort right back in her face.

The waves crashed against all sides of *The Sweet Tooth* as the giants churned the waters, marching to the cynocephaly who had promised the return of their son. Axel pointed his boat to lead them south—toward Los Angeles.

The wind bellowed against them from the west, pushing *The Sweet Tooth* dangerously close to horizontal, so that if Bailey or Savannah were to reach down on the opposite side, their fingers would touch the water. As they shortened the distance between themselves and Axel, Bailey readied a Frisbee, although he knew that even he would not be able to overcome the force of the wind and his Frisbee would fly uselessly into the water.

"You're going to have to throw me when we're close enough," he said to Nikos. "I have to get on that boat."

But Nikos was pointing south, and now Bailey and Savannah could see it—a looming black shadow in stark contrast to the gray storm clouds. It was large and round like an alien obsidian moon rising from the ocean.

"Is that another sea giant?" Savannah gasped.

"Maybe it's a battleship," Bailey suggested.

Nikos shook his head. "I hope you are wrong, young Buckleby. A battleship would be no match against a sea giant. If Pazuzu tells the giants their son is threatened by a human-made machine, they will simply scoop up the ship in their hands and throw it at the nearest human city, killing millions. I would hope your human leaders have learned their lesson after San Francisco."

A V-formation of fighter jets raced ahead of them, searing the sky with plumes of exhaust and a roar that filled their ears, even drowning out the wind and the ocean. To the west, up in the clouds that obscured the great titans, orange and black explosions blossomed, and Bailey heard the sea giants scream for the first time. Their cries droned out the boom of the jets, and they all had to put their hands to their ears. Savannah pointed with an inaudible *Look!* as a fighter jet spiraled and splashed into the ocean. Soon after, they saw the parachute of the pilot who had ejected. He disappeared into the blur of clouds and water, and Bailey wondered if he would drown out there. The other four jets circled in and out of the dark belt of clouds, as if they were mosquitoes seeking a vulnerable spot of giant skin. But the giants swatted at them like the tiny annoyances they were. The fighter jets buzzed and circled one more time and then raced back to the east to regroup.

"Sea giants are peaceful," Nikos said. "They mean humans no harm. They only want their son returned to them."

"DID YOU SEE THAT?" Pazuzu's voice echoed

across the water. He stood
on the stern with one fist
up, his pointed ears
pushed back by the wind.
His sloop rocked back
and forth, but he stood
tall and straight and easy,
as if the boat were nothing
but an oversized surfboard.
"I WILL TELL THE
GIANTS YOU MEAN TO
KIDNAP THEIR BABY
AGAIN! I WILL TELL
THEM TO CRUSH
YOU! YOU WILL
ALL BE DROWNED!
TURN BACK, HUMANS!"

"He's telling the truth," Nikos said grimly. "He could command the giants to destroy whatever or whomever he pleases."

"You're going to have to throw me over to his boat," Bailey said again.

"Me first!" Savannah screamed into the wind. Bailey shook his head no, but he really did want her help. How could he defeat this mad cynocephaly alone?

Nikos looked horrified but also realized there was nothing else to be done. As *The Sweet Tooth* pulled within just twenty feet of the demon's boat and thunder cracked right over their heads, the sea giants' legs lifted and came ever closer. Nikos picked up Bailey with both of his hands and prepared to twirl around and shot-put him over.

"Okay!" Bailey yelled. "DO IT!"

Nikos almost did throw Bailey, but the cynocephaly reappeared on his deck, pulling Bailey's blindfolded and handcuffed father behind him. He threw Dougie down to the deck, belly first, and lifted his megaphone.

"DO YOU WANT YOUR FATHER TO LIVE?"

Of course Bailey did, but before he could answer, the wind demon put one foot on his father's back and gave him a strong push.

"THEN GO GET HIM."

And Bailey's father slid headfirst, blindfolded and handcuffed, into the dark green water.

CHAPTER THIRTY-TWO

SHOULD A SON JUMP?

"**PUT ME DOWN!** Throw me in! Help me save him!" Bailey demanded. One of the goblins gave him a pair of goggles and he quickly put them on.

"Bailey, no. *Listen!*" Nikos pleaded. Mr. Boom stepped off the gas, and the cynocephaly's boat zigged and zagged toward the giants' legs, quickly getting away. He swung *The Sweet Tooth* around to Dougie, who took one final breath before sinking beneath a dark green wave.

Should a son jump into turbulent ice-cold water to save his drowning father? What if the son is barely one hundred pounds and the father well over three hundred? Even if he could swim down fast enough, how could he possibly pull him up? And of course his love for his father would prevent him from letting go, so *if* he were to jump and *if* he were able to swim down fast enough and *if* he were to grab hold of his sinking father's shirt, the outcome would be death for both of them. Bailey would drown with his father, so there would be *no one* to save poor kidnapped Henry, *no one* to return him to his giant parents, and *no one* to prevent all the people of all the coastal cities from being subjected to the wind demon's threats. So obviously, though it would be a horrible and difficult decision to make, the son should choose *not* to jump in to save his father.

But Bailey plunged into the water.

CHAPTER THIRTY-THREE

A PLEASANT DREAM TO COMFORT HIM WHILE HE DROWNED

BAILEY HELD ON to his Frisbee because there was nothing else he could do. A Frisbee in his hand prevented him from panicking, and he knew that if he panicked, he would only drown that much faster. His father had to be sinking below him, so he forced himself to somersault in the water, to kick his feet, and to dive down, down, down.

Was that him? The cold salt water swirled all around, but a bright green figure was floating toward him. Bailey dove in its direction, thinking, *If that's not him, I have to go up for air or die.*

Bailey's first delirious thought was that she was beautiful. She was pale with bright green eyes and blue lips and a halo of golden hair. Cold hands grabbed on to his so that he could only be still, could no longer kick, and so that she could kiss him on the mouth. The surprise of the kiss excited him, but he assumed he was dreaming or dying, because when she kissed him, he felt his lungs relax. Air rushed in; air flowed out. He inhaled, he exhaled, as if his body was breathing in rhythm with the golden-haired angel. Or demon. What was she? When her lungs emptied, his lungs filled, and she intertwined her arms with his so that his wrists crossed behind his back.

She pushed him down into the water, and with her green-and-gold-scaled tail flicking back and forth, she guided him deeper. Although he knew the water must be cold enough to kill him, he tingled with warmth. This surely was a dream.

Bailey could see his father sinking near him, and he felt horrible for having failed him. Blindfolded and handcuffed, his father was drowning. But suddenly Bailey saw twelve little scuba divers surround him. They each wore headlamps and were looping a nylon rope around his father's waist and under his armpits. Then, with all the force their little legs could muster, they swam upward. *How beautiful*, Bailey thought, *if only it were real*, because this was nothing more than a pleasant dream to comfort him while he drowned.

The girl gave him another breath, gripped his wrists tighter, and as she pulled Bailey deeper down, the goblins released the oxygen in their scuba tanks to shoot them up to the surface, pulling his three-hundred-pound father behind them. *That's good that Dad will be okay, because I'm going to go with this magical girl to the bottom of the ocean and see what no human has seen before. Is she a mermaid? Will she rip my heart out and eat it? If she does, will I feel it? Or will the cold water make me so numb that I won't feel a thing and I'll be able to watch her do it? She's so beautiful and glowing and her teeth look so sharp.*

A cloud of blood appeared in the water around him. *Is that my blood?* The mermaid was suddenly pushing him away and shaking her head violently back and forth. He saw her sharp white teeth flash in rage, her pale face with blue and green veins illuminated by a light above them. Her eyes shone green with anger as she extended her razor-sharp fingernails. But a blade jabbed through the water, piercing her hand. The mermaid shrieked with pain, turned away, and retreated to the dark depths below.

Savannah—she was wearing a wet suit, scuba gear, goggles, and a headlamp. She grabbed Bailey by his hoodie and pulled with all her strength. Then she put her scuba pack's rescue mouthpiece to Bailey's lips so he could breathe, although he wasn't feeling very much of anything at that moment except a blurry feeling of happiness, gratitude, and warmth, and absolutely nothing in his fingers and toes.

CHAPTER THIRTY-FOUR

ALIVE

NIKOS AND SAVANNAH wrapped Bailey in towels to warm him up and bring him back to life.

"Stay with us, son," he heard his father say. He was smiling down at Bailey, wrapped in towels himself.

"Dad," he said softly.

"You're my sweet, brave boy," he said proudly, hugging him tight and hurting him in the best possible way. They were surrounded by the twelve goblins in wet suits.

Bailey couldn't believe these goblins and his father weren't trying to kill each other. As if they read his thoughts, one of the smaller ones said, "You saved the stars, we saved your father, and now we will *all* save the baby sea giant together."

Capella stepped forward and gave Bailey a dry towel. "I know you and your father don't speak the sea giants'

language, but maybe we can make them understand—
somehow—that just like their son belongs with them, the
stars belong in the sky. Maybe if we help them, they will
help us."

Capella seemed so earnest, and Bailey was so cold, all
he could do was nod. But the wind demon still had Henry.

The sea giants had surfaced all the way to their torsos,
swinging their arms as they moved. The giants looked
more like massive blue skyscrapers than living things. To
the southwest, the dark mysterious half-moon that was
looking less and less like a battleship was getting bigger
and closer.

Bailey's father came close and knelt next to his son.
"Bailey," he said quietly, his eyes wet from both salt water
and real tears, "I didn't know any greater pain until I
walked downstairs to find you kidnapped—my only son
and greatest joy stolen from me. The pain made me want
to do anything to get you back. Now I know how much
Henry's parents must have suffered for an unbearably long
seven years. No wonder they smashed San Francisco into
rubble. I feel so guilty for being the cause of that and having kept Henry from them for that long."

He hugged his son close and Bailey was starting to feel
warm and alive again.

"You've done such a good job. I'm so proud of you, but
you don't need to chase this evil cynocephaly one minute
more. I'll take over. Monster hunting with you is great
fun, but maybe I showed you my dangerous world too
early. Maybe you should concentrate on being a boy for as

long as you can. I can fight this wind demon myself and rescue Henry."

Bailey shook his head. "No, Dad. We'll stop him together. We both love Henry that much."

His father smiled his big gorilla smile, swept the wet shag of hair out of his eyes, and held Bailey by the shoulders.

"Son, it's not necessary. As soon as we get close enough, I'm going to blow his boat to smithereens with dynamite."

"Dad, no, please. That will hurt Henry. I keep telling you—dynamite won't solve all of our problems."

His father patted Bailey on the cheek. "Not if I time it just right. Maybe if I throw a stick at the top of the mast— or maybe the mainsail. Not to worry, boy. I'll blow up what's necessary when the time is right."

"Dad, listen to me—"

But they had gained on Axel, who was facing them on his bow with his megaphone.

"WOULD YOU GUYS PLEASE STOP FOLLOWING ME? YOU ARE REALLY STARTING TO CREEP ME OUT!"

Dougie stood up tall and determined, his eyes focused on his enemy.

"Candycane, where do you keep your dynamite?"

Without taking his hands from the steering wheel, Candycane called over his shoulder, "There's no dynamite on this boat."

"What?" Bailey's father shouted, as if going out to sea

without dynamite was as absurd as leaving the house without pants.

"DO YOU GUYS REALLY THINK YOU CAN STOP ME? THESE AREN'T THE ONLY GIANTS I COMMAND!" Axel bellowed. Then he made a haunting and strange hum that Bailey had never heard a dog or a human make before. It sort of sounded like— *"WAHOOOOOOOM."*

The dark half-moon to the west began to rise. To Bailey, it looked like a massive black wall, slick and speckled with barnacles. The thing kept rising and rising, and a great fountain of water burst into the air from its topside. And then two unbelievably enormous eyes, each bigger than *The Sweet Tooth* itself, began to open.

The black wall was alive.

Dougie could not help but gasp like a child— a child who had never stopped marveling at the magnificence and terror of monsters. The Bucklebys had been selling driftwood figurines of the great beast in their souvenir shop for years, but here it was in real life, in the flesh.

"The Great Whale," his father said with pure wonder. "Just like the one that swallowed our people years ago. As real as real can be."

"You did not pay me for this!" Candycane roared above the sound of the motor and the waves crashing against the yacht, but even he could only admire the mighty beast as it completely surfaced.

Then its mouth began to open, and as it did, water rushed in, and with it *The Sweet Tooth*. The whale had great yellow teeth and the biggest gray tongue that looked like an endless pulsating carpet.

"Galloping Gertrude," Mr. Boom groaned. "I never thought I'd die like this."

Savannah brandished her sword before her and said, "We are Whalefatians. We have survived whale swallowing before!"

Dougie patted her on the back. "You speak the truth, orphan girl. We were made for this. Hold on tight, everybody!"

As *The Sweet Tooth* was sucked into the great mouth, and Axel once again began to put distance between himself and his pursuers, Candycane tried to turn the yacht around, to no avail. The tip of the humongous tongue lifted *The Sweet Tooth* up and out of the water.

He turned off the motor, and for an impossibly long pause, they all waited to be swallowed. But instead of disappearing down the terrifyingly dark throat, the great tongue held them up in the air. Despite the storm swirling around them, the crew of *The Sweet Tooth* found themselves in a space of calming quiet.

Then a voice so familiar to Bailey, even after six and a half years, called out cautiously from somewhere deep within the whale.

"Hello?"

CHAPTER THIRTY-FIVE

GEORGE

BAILEY TIPTOED SLOWLY to the bow of the yacht, peering into the darkness. The whale's breath was hot and humid and stank of dead fish, but he walked through the thick air as if it were harmless fog. He searched the shadows for the person he now knew was alive, deep in there somewhere.

"*Mom?*" His voice cracked. The goblins, Nikos, Savannah, and Bailey's father slowly walked to the bow of the yacht, too.

After a long pause, they all heard her echo back. "Oh, Bailey, my sweet everything, it's really you!"

He saw a faint silhouette of a woman at the base of the whale's long tongue—he knew it was her.

"Mom," Bailey cried. "I thought you were dead."

"No, my perfect prince, I'm not dead. I couldn't die

without seeing you become a man. Though perhaps you already have. You certainly are brave to try to stop a cynocephaly way out here in the middle of the Pacific Ocean. I'm so proud of you for trying to protect the human race from two very misunderstood sea giants. I've thought of you every day for six and a half years and missed you so, so much."

"Katrina," his father said urgently, holding the yacht railing tight.

"Dougie? Oh, Dougie, how wonderful to hear the voice of my big, sweet husband! Knowing I am so close and yet so far from my two favorite men just makes my predicament all the more frustrating."

"Katrina, my sweet darling! We have to get you out of there!"

"Well, easier said than done, my sweet husband. Every time I try to swim out of here, or even walk to the tip of his tongue, this big friend of mine swallows me back in. He's a very lonely whale, and perhaps it's to my own detriment that I learned his language, because he's only a young, endangered creature with no one to talk to. I've tried to steer him back to Whalefat Beach many times, but he doesn't want to lose me as a conversation partner. We've been searching the seas to find him a possible mate, but there aren't very many giant female whales out on the dating scene. So although I've been so sad that he hasn't returned me to you both, I've tried very hard to be his friend. Everyone needs a friend—even George."

"Who's George?" Bailey asked.

"This whale is George! He seems like a George to me with his big forehead and yellow teeth, so that's the name I've given him."

At hearing his own name, George blew a geyser of salt water up and out of his blowhole that showered down on all of them.

"That horrible Axel Pazuzu has commanded George to swallow you all whole," his mother said.

"Well, if it is our fate to be swallowed, then so be it," his father said. "Whalefatians are quite adept at living inside whales."

Mr. Boom interrupted. "I don't particularly like the sound of that!"

"No," Katrina said. "I've asked George not to listen to that evil wind demon, even though he promised to find him a girlfriend. I reminded George that millions of innocent children just like him would be terribly hurt if you all weren't allowed to return Henry to his parents. And George, I am proud to say, knows to do the right thing, because he has a very, very big heart."

His father stood up on the rail of *The Sweet Tooth* in desperation. "Darling, I was so greedy. I was so stubborn—I wanted Henry to be a rare Swiss troll so badly, I wasn't willing to listen to the truth. I refused to believe anything to the contrary. But you were right as usual. Every night since, I've wished I could ask your forgiveness. Worst of all, everyone in San Francisco had to pay the price for *my* foolishness."

"Oh, Dougie," his mother's voice echoed. "You just

really love monster hunting, that's all! Your passion is why I have always loved you, but sometimes passion makes one do really, really stupid things. You mustn't beat yourself up about it."

Even though he was cold and shivering and Axel was getting away, Bailey pretended he was warm under the illuminated, baby-blue blanket. Some would do just about anything for gold, or to save the stars, or to find a female whale companion. But Bailey wanted only one thing at that moment—to have his mother back.

"I'm coming in after you," Bailey said. "We'll figure out how to get out together."

"Bailey," his mother said sweetly, "I would give almost anything to hold you tight again. And this is so hard for me to say, but you're a young man now, so I think you will understand. We can't always think of ourselves. There are so many creatures in the world that need love, and Bucklebys are very good at finding the ones that need it most. When George is a little older, I think he will understand, too. He will let me go when the time is right."

"But, Mom," Bailey said, "*I'm* your son, not George."

"You are, Bailey," his mother said so sadly. "And that's why I'm asking so much of you."

Suddenly George let loose another huge fountain of salt water from his blowhole, and his mouth began to slowly shut. He bellowed, "*Wahoooooooom!*"

"But, George," Katrina cried, "must we leave so soon? Let us stay a few moments longer."

"*Wahoooooooom! Wahoooooooom!*"

Bailey heard his mother choke back a lonely sigh. "George says that if I was serious about you saving Los Angeles from being stomped, then we should part company right now. And although I don't want to admit it, my beautiful Bailey, he's quite right."

"But, Mom," Bailey protested, wanting to say anything that would keep her here with them. "Just run out of there right now—George can follow us and we can all be together!"

"I wish I could, my sweet prince, but George is stubborn that way." Even before Bailey's mother could say more, George began to descend. The whale flicked his tongue between his great yellow teeth, setting *The Sweet Tooth* gently on the water. Dougie climbed over the rail to stand on the tip of the bow.

"Dad, what are you doing?" But Bailey already knew.

"Son," he said, smiling, taking one hand off the rail to place it on Bailey's shoulder. "I can't abandon your mother a second time. You've grown up to be such a smart monster hunter and the best son a father could ask for. I know *you* can get Henry back and do the right thing. Deep down, did I believe what your mother knew? That he was the son of two sea giants who were grieving his disappearance? I don't know, maybe I did. But all of this doesn't excuse my ignorance of the facts. You didn't ignore the facts. You faced the facts dead-on, Bailey, and you did what was right and very, very difficult—you confronted your father. I need to do the right thing for once in my life—I need to save your mother."

"No, Dougie," his mother said harshly. *"Don't you even think it.* You have to stay with Bailey. You're all he's got to protect him, to feed him, to clothe him, to love him, and to make sure he flosses on a regular basis. No son of mine will go through life without rigorous dental hygiene. Don't you worry, my sweet husband. I'll get out of here someday—I mean, I think I will—I just need to wean George off my friendship like I weaned our son off a pacifier many years ago."

His father squeezed Bailey's shoulder, giving him that familiar pain. "I hate to leave you to fight that rotten Pazuzu alone, but I promise I won't be gone for long. I'll talk your mother into a whale-breakout and we'll be home before you know it." His eyes were pleading, as if he needed his son to confirm that this really was the right decision.

Bailey could hear Capella sniffling behind him, and even Savannah's eyes were beginning to well up with tears.

"Dad, I don't know what to do. How can I possibly stop a wind demon with just a Frisbee?" Bailey felt utterly alone.

His father took his hand off Bailey's shoulder. "You're not just a boy with a Frisbee. You can outthink any monster in the world. Now, my beautiful baby boy, prove me right. Go do what your father failed to."

George winked at them with his huge left eye as he sank lower and lower, his mouth closing and water rushing in. He bellowed again, *"Wahooooooom!"*

"Bailey! Bailey! One more thing!" his mother cried.

"Mom?"

"Have you met any nice girls?"

Bailey turned red and didn't say a word. Savannah leaned forward and shouted into the whale's mouth. "Yes, ma'am, he has!"

"Are you a mermaid, young lady?"

Bailey spoke up. "No, Mom. She's not."

"My sweet prince, I like her already."

Dougie flexed his knees, getting ready to jump. "I have to do this, son. Are you going to be okay? You *have* to tell me you're going to be okay."

Bailey could see the pain in his father's eyes. He knew that if he really wanted to, he could say *No*, and his father would stay on *The Sweet Tooth*. One word, and his father would change course. But instead, knowing how much his father loved his mother, and how much he himself loved her, and that he had only one real memory of his mother to shield him from the darkness, Bailey said *Yes*.

His father leaned forward and kissed Bailey on the forehead. "Bailey, my son, have faith in your old man. Whalefatians are very good at escaping giant whales—we proved that a very long time ago, and we will prove it again." He squeezed Bailey's shoulders one last time and then cried, "Katrina! I'm coming! Alley-oop!"

His father launched himself off the rail, and like a perfectly graceful gorilla, landed feetfirst on the tip of the whale's tongue. George's mouth closed around Bailey's father, the water frothing around the whale as he turned to dive beneath the waves. Bailey stepped off the rail of the bow and swept the wet shag of hair out of his eyes. In the distance, to the south, he could see the cynocephaly's little sailboat zigzagging toward the marching giants. Time was running out.

CHAPTER THIRTY-SIX

MAN TO DOG

THEY WERE LESS than a mile from the giants when they drew near to the wind demon's boat. As *The Sweet Tooth* got closer, they saw that Axel had a leaf blower strapped to his body. He was blowing air into the sails.

"That cynocephaly really isn't all that bright," Nikos said as they approached.

"Get ready to throw me over there," Bailey said, coming up from the galley where he had been concocting a secret plan with the goblins. He stuffed as many Frisbees as he could in his hoodie and tried to push his parents out of his mind. If he thought about them, he would worry they were drowned or digested or worse. An expert monster hunter had to work on one problem at a time, and the current problem was getting aboard the wind demon's boat without dropping anything he was carrying.

Axel raised his megaphone again. "YOU'VE RUN OUT OF TIME. TURN BACK. THESE GIANTS ARE MINE TO COMMAND!"

The minotaur picked up Bailey and raised him high over his head as Candycane pulled *The Sweet Tooth* as close as he dared to the demon's sloop. Taking in a mighty bull breath, Nikos yelled, "GO!" as he threw Bailey across.

Savannah shouted, "Go get 'em, Bailey boy!"

Axel blasted Bailey right in the face with his blower, trying to blow Bailey off his boat as if he were nothing more than a dried leaf. Bailey rolled and jumped to his feet. The cynocephaly stared him down with true malice, his bad eye pulsating underneath the eye patch.

"Tell me, Bailey. Where is your father to protect you now? Under the sea?"

"Yes," Bailey said defiantly.

"Eaten by mermaids?"

"By a whale."

The wind demon smirked cruelly. "Well, as long as *something* ate him. You will have a worse fate, of course. Death by drowning is an awfully painful way to go."

At the bow of the boat, Bailey saw Henry in chains. The baby sea giant's tongue wagged happily when he saw his friend, and he pulled hard against his shackles to run over to him. Realizing he was stuck, Henry cried a long and mournful *roooooooump!*

In rapid sequence, Bailey fired three Frisbees. *Pft, Pft,* and *Pft!* Axel fended them off with his leaf blower, redirecting the Frisbees out to sea.

"They don't call me a wind demon for nothing."

Bailey fired three more. *Pft, Pft, Pft.* But again, Pazuzu blew them away.

"Is it to be hand-to-hand combat, then?" the wind demon barked.

"Yes!" Savannah landed on the sloop with her sword drawn. She was very lucky she didn't cut herself as she rolled up onto her feet. Bailey tried to stop her—he had a secret plan after all—but she charged Axel straight on.

Pazuzu cranked his leaf blower up to SUPER HIGH and blasted.

Savannah had to close her eyes when the hot airstream hit her, which was long enough for Axel to drop the leaf blower, grab her wrists, and twist the sword out of her hands. He held the steel blade to her neck as she clawed at his arm.

"I don't want to hurt your very brave but very foolish girlfriend, Bailey Buckleby. Now, listen. You've tried your best tonight and I commend you for it. But I have three thousand years of experience on you, and I intend to live the rest of my long years in comfort. So, cut your losses, monster hunter. Leave now before you lose more than just your parents. I'll be taking Henry, and I will make you humans pay for killing so many of my people."

Bailey took a tentative step forward. "And you think humans should pay *you*?"

"Yes, of course," Axel said smugly. "Three billion in gold will do. *For now.*"

Bailey winced at how close the wind demon was holding the sword to Savannah's neck. She struggled in his grip, and he worried that if she struggled too much, she'd give herself a horrible, possibly fatal, wound. Bailey put up a hand to try to convince them both to remain calm.

"Fight him, Bailey!" Savannah shouted as she tried unsuccessfully to elbow her captor in the gut. She was stronger than Bailey, and he knew that if she couldn't fight the cynocephaly off, neither could he. Frisbees weren't going to solve this—he was going to have to use his wits.

"You are three thousand years older than me, Mr. Pazuzu, which should make you that much smarter. That's why I'm surprised you've made so many stupid, stupid—*I mean really stupid*—decisions."

Axel clicked his tongue. "You have a lot of nerve, Bailey. I'm about to make three billion dollars in gold while you find yourself alone on the ocean with no parents and your girlfriend's life in my hands. And *I'm* the stupid one?"

Bailey shifted the weight he was carrying in his hoodie pocket. "Cynocephali are supposed to be so brilliant at business, but I've heard about your past investments. You seem to be better at losing money than making it. Holiday sweaters for dogs and cats? I'm only in the seventh grade, but that has to be the dumbest idea I've ever heard."

Even with her own sword at her throat, Savannah laughed. "You've got to admit, that *is* pretty stupid, Mr. Dog-head."

"Hey!" Axel protested, tightening his grip on Savannah's wrist. "Humans love the holidays and humans love cats and dogs. How was I to know humans aren't ashamed to let their pets run around naked—even on Christmas!"

"And now look what you're doing," Bailey said carefully, daring to take one more step. He could see Henry behind them, pulling against his chains. "You're going to demand humans pay you three billion dollars. And maybe the mayor of Los Angeles will even give it to you. But then what? You'll have two sea giants following you wherever you go, because they'll still want their son back. You'll have to make up a story that he's in *another* city, and you'll have to sail there as fast as you can. Then you'll have to tell another lie, and another lie. And don't think our navy won't be following you the whole time. And *me*. I'll be right there behind you, too. You say you want to live in comfort, but you'll never get a moment's rest. Not one free moment to sleep, to windsurf, or do anything fun with all of your gold because you'll be constantly on the move. You'll be a prisoner to your own stupid, *stupid* scheme."

Axel's cunning dog grin started to turn. "I'm not stupid. Cynocephali have superior intellects to every other race on this planet—*especially humans.*"

Bailey knew he had the wind demon on the run. "You haven't thought this through, have you? You know what else you've forgotten? Henry eats a whole chicken in a bowl of water three times a day, *every day*. Better get a bigger boat with a freezer full of chickens if you're going to go through with this!"

Axel Pazuzu's whiskers twitched with frustration. "Well, then. Fine! I'll give Henry back to his parents after Los Angeles is destroyed and I'll still have my three billion!"

Bailey shrugged. "Okay. You could do that. But then you won't have two sea giants to use as a threat against humans. Do you think they'll just let you sail away with three billion in gold bars because you earned it? No, the police will come after you. The FBI will come after you. Maybe Mr. Boom will come after you, too. And I'll still be on your tail—*until the day I die*. No peace for Axel Pazuzu. No, sir, Mr. Wind Demon. You *will* be a wind demon, because you'll be forced to blow here and there and everywhere, carrying around a load of gold somehow. You're going to need a *real* pet troll to carry your bags. Yes, Mr. Pazuzu, you sure are smart."

Savannah was giggling.

"Hey!" Axel snapped. "You think you're so clever? What do you know? You're just a kid that sells monsters and souvenirs!"

Now Bailey had him.

"That's right, *wind demon*," he said, "I *do* know the monster business. I'm a Buckleby and my father has taught me well. That's why I'm going to offer you exactly what Henry is worth, no strings attached."

Bailey threw a cloth bundle of stones onto the deck—Pazuzu's dog ears pointed straight up.

"Are those what I think they are?"

Bailey shrugged. "See for yourself."

Without taking his one good dog eye off him, Axel ripped the bundle open with the tip of Savannah's sword. Shiny golden nuggets spilled out before them.

"How much is there?" he asked, unable to hide his greed.

"It's not three billion, but it's enough to make up for all the mistakes you've made. Think about it," Bailey said shrewdly, the ocean wind whipping in his face. "You can take this gold and leave without Henry, but *only if* you promise never to bother the sea giants or the goblins or anyone in California ever again. If you agree to that, you won't be chased by anyone, not even me. You can stay on permanent vacation for all I care. Do whatever you want. Waste your time selling iceberg vacation homes—as long as you stay far away from here."

"Hey! They were luxury Arctic adventure spas and they were beautiful! But humans are heating up the planet and all the northern ice is melting. It's *your* fault that my vacation rentals sank into the sea!" Axel squinted at Bailey's hoodie pocket, gesturing at it with Savannah's sword. "I see you've got more in the bank."

Bailey shrugged and threw out a second bundle. "That's my final offer. Take it and go."

Savannah whistled. "That looks like a lot of gold, Mr. Dog-head."

"I know that!" he snapped at her, and Bailey could almost feel Pazuzu's greed. "But I see you still have more for me," he said.

Bailey stared him down, pretending he was over his limit so the wind demon would think he had the upper hand.

"Come on," he said. "Do you want your sweet Henry back or not?"

Bailey threw out one last bundle.

"There. That's all the gold the goblins intended to give you to help them in their quest. That has to be over fifty pounds of gold for you to take if you just sail away. You know as well as I do that any respectable cynocephaly would take that offer. You are a failure of a salesdog if you refuse."

Axel chuckled. "You're too sure of yourself. I see there's more in your pocket."

Bailey patted his pocket carefully. "This last bundle is dynamite," Bailey answered calmly and without hesitation. "If you refuse this deal, I'll blow your boat out of the water. That's what my father would have done first thing."

Axel Pazuzu raised his one good hairy dog eyebrow, and Bailey stared him down. He knew the wind demon couldn't walk away from such easy money now. There was no need to offer a single cent more. His customer was already hooked.

Axel relaxed his grip on Savannah. "Do I have your

word—*man to dog*—that you won't chase me down? That you won't seek vengeance when I turn my back?"

Bailey put his hand out. "You have my word, and my word is gold."

Axel Pazuzu slowly let go, gave Savannah her sword, and shook Bailey's hand.

CHAPTER THIRTY-SEVEN

A BIG FAVOR

BAILEY BUCKLEBY, Savannah, a minotaur, Candycane Boom, twelve goblins, and a baby sea giant stood on the deck of *The Sweet Tooth* and watched the cynocephaly's yellow-sailed sloop fade away. Axel Pazuzu raised his megaphone to his lips and barked, "BYE, BYE." Seconds later, he was gone.

Mr. Boom wiped the water away from his bald head. "You know, you shouldn't negotiate with terrorists. Just how much gold was in those bundles?"

Bailey chuckled. "I don't know. Ask the goblins."

The goblins were eager to tell everybody their part in the ploy. "Most of the stones weren't gold," one said.

"Some of them were the fool's gold stones from my necklace," Capella said proudly.

"Some of them were my lucky painted rocks," another said.

"Some of them were my old teeth," a very wrinkled goblin said, putting a hand over his mouth because he had very few teeth left at all.

"He tricked us, so we tricked him back!" Capella said triumphantly, and they all started laughing.

Even Mr. Boom was impressed by the double-cross. "It won't take him long to figure out what you did. What will you do when he realizes he's been duped?"

"We will fight him once and for all!" Savannah said, lifting her sword into the sky.

"A few of the stones on top were real gold, and maybe that will be enough to keep him away. But I think," Bailey said thoughtfully, "that he's learned his lesson—that the ransom business is more trouble than it's worth. Besides, I'd guess that once we get Henry back home, his parents won't let a cynocephaly ever get near their baby boy again."

Ahead of them, the two grieving parents still marched south toward Los Angeles, searching for their lost son. The twelve goblins looked expectantly at Bailey.

"Are you going to keep your promise?" Canopus asked doubtfully.

"I'm going to keep both of my promises," Bailey said.

"And how do you propose to do that, human boy?"

Bailey wondered. *The Sweet Tooth* was bouncing higher and higher, and he was starting to feel seasick again. The sea giants' legs were visible to their knees now, but their heads were obscured in clouds. How good was their eyesight? Could they see this little boat one thousand feet below them? Their son was right here. How could Bailey tell them their baby boy was so, so close?

He shook his head. "There's only one thing to do."

Savannah nodded. "You have to try it."

They were both thinking the same thing.

"Nikos, can you help me lift Abigail's cage out of the cabin?"

They brought her cage up, and she flapped madly against the bars, complaining, *Chirp! Chirp, chiiiiiirp!*

Savannah stroked the harpy's stark white hair and whispered in her ear. "Listen to me, beautiful lady. I know you've never done this before, and it seems very scary, but it's the only way we can return a baby to his parents and save many more children in Los Angeles. And I promise Bailey will do you a big favor when we complete this very important mission."

Savannah raised her eyebrows expectantly at Bailey, and he sighed. He knew exactly what promise Savannah wanted him to make.

"Yes, Miss Abigail," he said. "If you will fly us up within eyesight of the giants, I will give you your freedom, and you can finally go home to your family in Greenland."

He wondered if she understood what he was offering. But when he saw her eyes well up with tears for a dream she'd nearly forgotten, he knew she understood perfectly.

Bailey removed two life jackets from the yacht's cargo space.

"I don't think there's room on her back for both of us," Savannah said.

"There isn't," Bailey agreed. "But there is enough space for me and one goblin." And he handed the other life jacket to Canopus.

CHAPTER THIRTY-EIGHT

SMALL

IN MOMENTS, *The Sweet Tooth* was nothing but a white speck on the water. Abigail flew up and up at such a steep angle that Bailey had to wrap his arms around her neck to keep from falling to his death. Canopus wrapped his arms around Bailey's chest so tight, he nearly choked the breath out of him.

As she circled upward, Bailey could see thousands of cars driving east and north to escape the incoming stomping sea giants, just like ants would march away from stomping humans. When Abigail reached a height of eight hundred feet above the water, Bailey pulled gently on her hair to guide her south toward the giants.

Eight hundred feet put them at shoulder height. Rain pelted their backs, and the wind threatened to push them off course, but despite being captive in a cage for two years,

Abigail showed expertise at navigating the thrusting stormy air currents. Bailey ducked his head down to keep the wind out of his face as he tried to think how he might tell the giants that Henry wasn't being held captive in Los Angeles but instead waited happily aboard a little boat just below them, if they only would take a moment to look.

We are nothing but mosquitoes to them, Bailey thought. His shouts in their ears would be nothing more than an annoying buzz, and they most likely didn't understand a word of English.

He did have three Frisbees under his hoodie. Like a mosquito, he figured he would have to anger the giants just enough to distract them, and when they tried to swat him, he'd have to swoop down toward *The Sweet Tooth* so they could see their little boy. Or maybe smell him? Could sea giants smell? He couldn't remember what Dr. March had to say on the subject.

As they approached, he felt Canopus's grip around his belly tighten. The clouds and rain parted for a moment, and there they were—enormous blue arms swinging slowly back and forth. Their skin shone blue, slick with rain, speckled with barnacles, and they were clothed in seaweed. No wonder helicopters and jets could do nothing to them. Their torsos towered so high and wide that any human bullets or even missiles would feel like nothing more than wasp stings. Painful perhaps, but easily ignored.

He pulled back on Abigail's hair and she protested with a *Chirp!* But still she climbed. Bailey tried not to look down or fear would overtake him. As they flew up past the giants' shoulders, Canopus cursed, "Oh sweet stars," and the great heads came into view. When the giants had been nothing but dormant colossi beneath the sea, their foreheads had protruded above the water line to form the Farallon Islands. The shoreline water mark could still be seen across their temples. Like crowns, barnacles rimmed their heads, just below toupees of seagrass, jagged rocks, and sand. At first, Bailey couldn't distinguish between the father and the mother, but when Abigail flew level to their eyes, Bailey could tell instantly. Henry's mother's eyes were round and soft and streamed tears. And although she was much, much larger, Bailey saw that she had Henry's mouth, curling up at the edges. When they flew closer to the father, his eyes showed nothing but the desire for vengeance, and when he opened his great mouth and bellowed in angry frustration, he released a suffocating gas of dead fish and plankton.

"Now what?" Canopus yelled into Bailey's ear, but Bailey wasn't quite sure himself, although he decided that if either of the giants could be distracted from their grief, the mother would be more likely. The father's great furrowed blue brow made Bailey think he was too angry to pay attention to a small boy riding a small harpy.

Abigail dipped and swayed as they zoomed right in on Henry's big mama. Bailey readied a Frisbee. Even in this wind, he knew he had the skill to hit whatever target he wished. The giants' faces were so large, he thought he could at least make contact. But when they were within range of the mother's enormous cheek, he realized that a

Frisbee would brush her as lightly as air. Even if he threw it in her eye, it would be nothing but a speck of flying dust to her. Bailey felt helplessly small, and his chest tightened when he realized there was no one to ask for help. Without a mother or a father, he felt completely helpless.

But he *did* have Savannah. He carefully withdrew his phone from his life jacket. If he fumbled, his phone would fall and be lost forever. He began to text her: *Up in giant's face. Need idea.*

But he didn't press SEND.

Of course! How could he not have thought of it earlier? The answer was already in his hand.

CHAPTER THIRTY-NINE

ZZT

"GO FOR HER EAR," he yelled into Abigail's own ear, tucking his head down close to hers.

Abigail banked into the wind stream created by the giants' march, then quickly flew over the mother giant's great head. Then she dove straight down to curve around the mama's giant earlobe. Her gigantic ear resembled a human's in shape, with a dark inner canal extending past their sight. It had been just at the water line when the giants stood dormant in the Pacific, so her ear was rimmed with starfish, sea urchins, and barnacles. Moss covered the entire inside, and of course, appropriate for a giant that has been asleep for years, stalactites of earwax hung that would never, ever be Q-tipped.

"Inside, Abigail. Inside!" Bailey's heart pounded with

excitement. He had a plan, but also realized that he would be exploring what no other monster hunter had ever explored before. Abigail flew in, and even sad Canopus could not help whistling in awe. The ridges and canals of the ear formed pools and rivers. Ocean water swirled in crevices filled with all kinds of creatures that hadn't thought to escape before their tidal pool homes were lifted one thousand feet up.

"We need to go farther in," Bailey whispered determinedly in Abigail's ear. "It's the only way." The harpy nodded her head in understanding, which struck Bailey as such a human gesture.

The air calmed around them, and the moss-covered ear canal became darker as they flew deeper and deeper. "Just a little farther," Bailey yelled, surprising himself by the increased volume of his voice echoing in the giant's ear canal. Abigail let her black-and-white osprey wings stretch completely open as they glided into the black.

He had studied the human ear in human biology. If Bailey could assume the giant's ear was at all similar, they would soon be approaching the eardrum.

The ear canal echoed with the howl of the wind outside. Bailey heard splashing, too, and he whispered to Abigail to slow down. She banked and they glided silently, side to side. It was almost time to try his plan and hope for the best, but the sound of splashing water alarmed him.

Bailey turned on the flashlight app on his phone just in time. *Zzt!* He ducked as a spear went whizzing over his head.

"Keep down, Canopus!" Bailey yelled, his voice echoing all around him. "It's another freaking mermaid!"

Zzt! Another spear veered toward them from the illuminated mermaid. She screeched through sharp teeth and pulled another spear of hardened earwax from the canal wall.

"Swing right above her," Bailey whispered into Abigail's ear. It didn't take much volume for the harpy to hear him now, and she agreed reluctantly with a most serious *chirp*.

Zzt! Abigail banked just before the spear nearly pierced the pointy tip of Canopus's long ear. Bailey had his three Frisbees ready, and Abigail dove in for the bombing run. Holding the phone flashlight in his left hand, he stood up as much as he dared, holding himself steady on Abigail with his knees and gripping all three Frisbees between the fingers of his right hand.

Pft! Frisbee to the forehead. *Pft!* Frisbee to the forehead. *Pft!* Frisbee to the forehead! Then *Zzt!* Her last wax spear flew wildly, and the mermaid screeched and dove out of her pool into the saltwater river of the ear canal to flee and tend to her likely concussion.

"Yeah!" Bailey and Canopus exclaimed together as loudly as they dared.

"Okay, girl," Bailey whispered. "Back around to the eardrum."

Bailey urged Abigail to fly in as close as they could. The ear canal narrowed on all sides—top and bottom, left and right. Soon the mother giant's ear canal was not much wider than Abigail's wingspan. Bailey patted her on her shoulder.

"Okay, girl. Take a rest."

She was grateful to do so. She circled and glided downward to softly land on the mossy canal floor, gently gripping the earwax below to hold them still. The canal ended in a thin blue membrane that curved with the canal wall. It vibrated with any motion they made.

Canopus sighed, ready for this aerial tour to be over. "Stopping for photos, eh?"

"No," Bailey said as quietly as he could, because he guessed the mother giant could now hear every word they breathed, every flap of Abigail's wings, every rustle of their life jackets. What would he do if she stuck her humongous finger in here and crushed them all? He turned off his phone's flashlight, leaving them in darkness except for the soft glow of his phone's home screen. He had eighteen percent battery life left. He hoped it was enough.

Bailey scrolled through his phone settings, looking for the ringtone he had customized months ago. He turned up the volume as loud as his phone would allow. Then he set the ringtone to play in a loop. He held his phone up to the giant blue membrane.

They all felt the mother inhale a great gust of wind as she stopped in her march, caught off guard. Her whole body shook, and Abigail nearly lost her grip on the flesh beneath her. The mother had heard the joyful, innocent sound of her baby, lost to her for seven years, and Bailey smiled when he heard her unleash a great wail that could only be a cry of relief and joy. His phone echoed the booming bass-drum rhythm over and over again: *Roump, roump, roump. Roump, roump, roump. Roump, roump, roump.*

CHAPTER FORTY

A HAPPY, INCONVENIENT TRUTH

A GREAT MOAN of surprise vibrated through them as the father sea giant echoed the same wonderful but incredibly loud wail. Bailey thought the resulting sound waves might tear them apart as his teeth chattered and his hands trembled. He patted Abigail and pulled back on her hair to fly up and out of the ear canal. She was happy to oblige. Another moan shook her, sending her crashing into the mossy wall, but Bailey and Canopus managed to keep upright. Bailey kept his phone up in the air so the big mama could continue to hear her baby's voice: *Roump, roump, roump.*

And then they flew out of her giant ear into the open air.

Canopus pointed. The sea giants' great blue faces

moved as if in slow motion relative to Bailey, the creases in their skin like earthquakes, their expressions undeniably turning from anger to hope.

"Fly just ahead of them, Abby. We'll lead them back home."

Abigail chirped and his phone repeated a steady *roump, roump, roump,* undoubtedly softer to the parents' ears now, but their heads turned slowly left and right trying to catch their baby's voice on the wind. Bailey had to multitask. He prayed he wouldn't drop his phone while pulling Abigail's hair to bank them toward the spot where the Farrallon Islands were supposed to be. He stopped Henry's bark from looping for just a moment to quickly call Savannah, holding on with his knees and trying not to let fear overtake him as he looked down to see the water churning around the giants' knees hundreds of feet below him.

"Bailey!" she screamed in delight.

"They're turning," he said excitedly. "Head north with Henry to where the islands are supposed to be and we'll let them meet there. I'm playing Henry's bark and they're following me!"

"You're a genius," she said, but in the background Bailey heard Mr. Boom shout out, "The time on our contract is almost up, buddy!"

"You will make an exception if we are an hour late," he heard Nikos say.

"Full speed!" Savannah cried. "You did it, Bailey boy!"

"*We* did it," he said, and he hung up to continue the *roump, roump, roump* loop as the giants turned completely about-face and followed. Helicopters buzzed behind them, not sure what to do. They must have seen a boy and a goblin flying on a harpy by now, but as of yet, they hadn't tried to shoot them down.

The giants followed the faint sound from Bailey's phone. They marched so slowly, he often had to turn Abigail around to circle back, gliding through the air currents around their heads, his phone barking *roump, roump, roump* just in front of their noses. It took so long for them to take a step in the direction he wanted, he didn't dare waste time letting them wonder which way to go. The helicopters buzzed like angry wasps behind them all, and Bailey imagined pilots and ground control arguing over protocols and authorization to use force and whether or not these giants were real. He imagined that, even now, generals and politicians miles from here were inventing stories to convince the public that monsters *still* did not exist, no matter what they might be seeing with their very own eyes.

Night had fallen over the West Coast and Bailey said, "Canopus, I think I can fulfill my promises to you now."

The goblin sighed and grumbled beneath his breath, clearly doubting him. Bailey pulled gently back on Abigail's hair. She turned upward, and they climbed through the wind. The moon in the distance barely revealed itself, nothing more than the thinnest crescent.

"Look up," Bailey said over his shoulder.

"Why?" Canopus sighed.

But then the little goblin saw.

The ambient city light could not hide them. Neither could the clouds, nor the moonlight. The stars lit up the entire sky from California to Japan, too many to count. The Milky Way—one long, graceful, illuminated brushstroke—stretched in a beautiful arc above them. Bailey heard Canopus's soft groaning.

"Sweet, beautiful stars," the pointy-eared goblin said. "There are so many of them! I never imagined—"

The goblin's voice trailed off as he looked up in absolute wonder. As Abigail spread her wings to glide, the hum of helicopters far behind them and the slosh of the ocean around the giants' feet way below them, Bailey felt as if they drifted through heaven. He supposed that, in a way, the stars and the wash of the Milky Way did look like a million, billion desk lamps and chandeliers lit by God in the greatest living room of all. It was so quiet, too, with only the occasional hopeful moan of the sea giant parents to remind them they were not alone with the stars.

"So, so many," Canopus repeated in awe. "They must have multiplied. They must be the children of the children of the stars. How did they escape the humans, I wonder."

The scientific part of Bailey couldn't help himself. "They never needed to escape, Canopus! That's what I wanted you to see. The stars have been safe all along. They are far, far away from Earth, safe from humans or anyone else."

Bailey could feel Canopus's arms shaking around his chest. The little goblin may have been cold, or quietly crying from the sight of all his beloved stars shining bright and free. It really was sad, Bailey thought, that ambient light hides the stars, and that human governments hide monsters. He felt very fortunate, even if he was an orphan now, that he was one of the few humans on the planet to have seen both worlds up close—and he had been changed forever by them.

After a very long moment, the goblin stopped shaking and exhaled. "I thank you for showing me this great beauty, Bailey. But if you could take me back to Capella, I would appreciate it. It's time for us to go home and return to our work."

Bailey wasn't sure if he had heard Canopus right. "But don't you see? You don't have to worry now. Your people don't need to be star guardians anymore. The stars are just fine without you. You don't need to risk your lives to steal electric lights, because the stars live! Doesn't that make you happy?"

The goblin sighed sadly. "Just the opposite, human boy. My life has been a complete waste of time, devoted to a mission that I now see has been completely meaningless. I suppose you're right—the stars never needed us. What will I live for now? I won't dare tell any of the Order about this. I will tell them you showed me the sky and it was black and empty. I won't take the meaning out of the lives of my people or make them feel hollow and foolish like I feel now. I guess the mountain goblins were right to migrate up into the snow where they could see the stars. I had always thought of them as traitors, but apparently they were right after all. Am I supposed to leave my people and join them? It's awfully cold in the mountains. I don't know what I will do. Maybe I'll take a mining job in Utah, or crawl into my bed and sleep for three weeks."

The goblin said no more, and when Bailey looked over his left shoulder, he saw Canopus wasn't even looking at the stars anymore. Instead, his head was tucked down into the back of Bailey's life jacket.

"I promised the twelve of you something else, too," Bailey said quietly. "I promised if you gave me the gold nuggets you intended for Pazuzu, I would ask the sea giants to lift the stars back up into the sky. Maybe it was deceptive of me, but I knew if I showed you that the stars were fine, you wouldn't need me to fulfill the second promise."

The goblin stopped him with a pat on the back. "It's fine, human boy. No apology necessary. I'm glad the stars are safe. It's a happy, inconvenient truth, which I will keep to myself. In time, I will tell my comrades that you asked, but that the giants said that even they could not lift the stars so high. The Eighteenth Goblin Order of Star Guardians will carry on and try to find another way."

For some reason Bailey felt guilty when he had expected to feel like a hero. He pulled gently on Abigail's hair to send them into a slow dive.

He pointed his phone at the giants so they wouldn't lose him and replayed the loop of *roump, roump, roump*. His phone only had seven percent battery life left, and he hoped he had timed this right. *The Sweet Tooth* came into view as he flew Abigail down to waist height of the giants.

Like an expert fighter pilot, he guided the harpy in line with the moving yacht, where he saw Nikos, Savannah, and Capella on deck with Henry bouncing excitedly next to them. Mr. Boom had turned on all of the yacht's lights so they'd be an easy target.

"Nice and easy, Abby," Bailey whispered as she glided in. She touched onto the deck with the softest of landings, her talons clicking lightly on the wood. Bailey climbed down and detached Canopus from his back. He put his hand on Abigail's shoulder and said, "Thank you," as Savannah moved closer to hug the proud bird-woman. But before she could, and before Bailey could even step back, Abigail launched straight up in the air and screeched *chiiiiiirp*, pointing herself toward Greenland.

"She didn't even wait to take a sardine break," Savannah said sadly, squinting her eyes to find the harpy in the dark night sky, but Abigail was already gone. "I hope she finds other harpies."

Roump, roump, roump, Bailey's phone kept barking. He told Candycane to slow the yacht down when they approached the site of the Farrallon Islands. "We're just about there," he said.

The yacht bounced up and down as the giants' footsteps came closer and closer, making the waves surge ever higher.

"Okay," Bailey said. "If we're going to do this, we should do it now."

Henry bounced on both his hands and feet in excitement. It was time for a new game as far as he was concerned.

Savannah jumped up and wrapped her arms around his neck.

"I'm going to miss you, Big Blue!"

The twelve goblins lined up and quietly patted him on the knees, each offering him a sweet goodbye. "Thank your parents for us," and "We honor you," and "The stars will bless you." Although when it was Canopus's turn, he couldn't say a word.

"Okay, anytime now," Candycane said urgently, trying to keep the bobbing yacht upright by pulling hard on the wheel. Each of the giant's steps caused a looming wave that any surfer would love to ride. Slowly, and with great gasping moans, the father and mother were beginning to lean over to get a closer look at the water. Boom's bald head was sweating. "We're really getting tossed around here, Bailey!"

Bailey scratched the back of Henry's neck and pulled his head down so that he could touch his forehead to the baby sea giant's.

"Okay, boy, it's time. I love you so much," he whispered. "So much so, that I need you to jump in the water now. You've been one of the best friends I've ever known, which is why I want you to have your parents back. I can't have mine, but I'm happy I can give you back to yours."

Henry replied with a *roump, roump, roump!* and licked Bailey's face, but the baby sea giant could not stop looking upward at his parents towering above him. He started bouncing on feet and hands in excitement, barking and whining with pure joy.

Bailey smiled. "Someday, Henry, you'll be that tall, too."

Then Bailey pushed Henry gently away from him. He gripped a neon-orange Frisbee in his right hand and pulled back slowly, like an Olympian readying to hurl a discus as far as humanly possible. He held his position as long as it took Henry to realize his old friend was going to throw the Frisbee way, way out there. Henry bounced up and down happily, always ready to play this game.

"Until we meet again," Bailey whispered, and with a perfect, graceful flick of the wrist, the Frisbee soared over the night green water. Henry never took his eyes off the disc, bounding for it using both hands and feet to gain speed, then leaping off the stern of *The Sweet Tooth* into the water. Bailey, Savannah, Nikos, and twelve goblins held the handrails and looked over the side as Henry swam a beautifully perfect butterfly stroke with the orange Frisbee in his mouth. He looked so proud.

"Hit the gas," Bailey said, his heart breaking, and Candy-cane did, turning the yacht toward Whalefat Beach.

Bailey watched Henry's bobbing blue head recede behind the yacht and it was hard not to cry leaving him there. But Henry would only be alone for a few moments. They all watched as two great giant heads descended out of the clouds, their hands on their knees, squinting their huge blue eyes as they looked for their baby in the water. As Henry disappeared from their view, they all heard the mother giant gasp a wonderfully happy "Ooomeeeeeee!"

Savannah smiled and said, "She found him."

Bailey felt a pride that he had never known before. He had fought off faeries, goblins, and even a wind demon, but better than those victories, he had reunited a child with his parents, and he could just feel that they would be a happy family of three for hundreds of years to come.

CHAPTER FORTY-ONE

TO HAVE A HAPPY LIFE

WHEN THE SEA GIANTS descended into the Pacific Ocean, the tops of their heads became the Farallon Islands again. There would be no press conference. Any rumors of just how close Los Angeles came to annihilation would be denied. All evidence to the contrary would be blamed on an imaginary earthquake.

Bailey missed Henry. Every day since he'd returned home, he sat on Whalefat Beach twirling a Frisbee on his finger, looking out at the waves. Way out there, Henry was underwater with his parents doing whatever sea giant families do. Did they play games? Did they hunt sharks and eels? Did Henry miss the whole raw chicken lunches the Bucklebys used to feed him? Maybe Bailey would visit him someday, or maybe their childhood friendship would be a nice memory for just a while, and they'd soon forget about each other altogether.

In a way, he was angry at Henry, and he knew that wasn't right. Henry had been reunited with his parents while Bailey had now lost both of his. It didn't seem fair.

Bailey still hoped that Buckleby and Son's Very Strange Souvenirs would one day again be a father-and-son business, but in the meantime, Bailey made the executive decision to sign on Nikos Tekton, the famous Labyrinthian of the Mojave Desert, and Savannah Mistivich, the sword-wielding heroine of the goblin tunnels. And if the citizens of Whalefat Beach called Nikos a freak or a demon or even a *monster*, then they would have to answer to *him*. Nikos was a bit apprehensive about taking such a public role in the business, but when Bailey told him his days of living in secrecy and shame were over, the minotaur couldn't help but smile.

"You do me a great honor, Bailey Buckleby."

They combined the leftover goblin gold to pay off Nikos's debt, which the minotaur tried to insist was not Bailey's concern. Bailey said, "We are business partners now, so it just makes good financial sense for us all to be debt-free."

"And Bullheads help Bullheads!" Savannah said proudly.

"Besides," Bailey said, "I have a very good idea that will require your special skills. It's an idea I think you're going to like."

There was still plenty of gold left over after paying Nikos's debt, and Bailey used it to purchase the store next to Buckleby and Son's Very Strange Souvenirs, which had been an unpopular hand-knitted sock shop for many years. Bailey wanted Nikos to transform the lot into the most artistic, most beautiful, most mind-challenging micro-maze he could imagine.

"Micro-maze?" Nikos asked, his eyes lighting up.

"Yes," Bailey said. "A micro-maze. A maze that has to fit into the small space next door. It can be only three stories high, and only as big as the lot, but it can have secret passages, and hidden levers, and trapdoors, and dark crawl spaces. Whatever you want. We could even hang faeries in lanterns throughout the maze to scare the crap out of customers. We'll connect the maze to our souvenir shop and charge twenty dollars for admission."

It was all Bailey had to say, because he and Savannah saw the light in Nikos's eyes burn bright as his minotaur brain started revving into high gear.

"It's an absolutely excellent idea," Nikos said happily, and he began drawing up the blueprints that very day.

Savannah taught introductory sword fighting in the shop on Tuesday and Thursday afternoons after school. She took lessons herself and had great plans to organize a Bullhead Brigade reunion. On other days, after school, she and Bailey went hunting for faeries.

One October Wednesday, Savannah suggested Bailey write an article about their adventure for *Peculiar*. He had never thought of himself as a writer, but he started working on a possible article during Mrs. Wood's class, because sometimes social studies wasn't all that exciting to a seventh grader who had flown into a sea giant's ear canal and lived to tell the tale.

After several weeks, his article for *Peculiar* nearly complete, he and Savannah had collected more than forty sugar-crazed faeries to sell in the infamous back room, and he was getting used to the idea that he might never see his parents again. He went to the beach every night to stare out at the ocean, but every night he returned to the store a little sooner than he had the night before.

"Listen," Nikos said one Saturday morning after cooking and serving Bailey a breakfast burrito, because it turned out Nikos was as skilled at making breakfast as he was at building mazes. "I want you to know how much I appreciate the life you've given me."

"I know," Bailey said.

"I want you to have a happy life, too."

"Thanks," Bailey said, barely looking at him, slightly embarrassed. "That's a nice thing to say." Bailey guessed that many orphans did have happy lives, but he figured if he was meant to be happy, it probably wouldn't happen until after high school. High school was an ugly obstacle for everyone—even kids with parents.

"I've been wanting to tell you something," Nikos said. "I threw the ratatoskers over the side of the yacht."

"What?" Bailey asked, even though he had heard the minotaur quite clearly. His mind was already racing.

"I threw the two ratatoskers into the whale's mouth as it was diving back into the sea. I did it really without thinking, but I guess I was hoping George would swallow them so that your parents would have a way of communicating with you. I don't know if the ratatoskers were swallowed or if they even survived. I didn't tell you until now because I didn't want you to expect anything, but I think maybe you could use a little bit of hope."

Bailey smiled politely and said, "Thanks." Nikos had given him a nice fantasy. He liked the idea of his parents penning a message on a very tiny piece of paper to pierce on a ratatosker tusk to deliver to him. But did they have an article of his clothing so the rodents could pick up his scent? Did they even have paper and pen? Bailey doubted it, and the ratatoskers had probably drowned or been eaten by sharks or speared by mean-spirited mermaids.

But at night, under his baby-blue blanket, he thought about this remote possibility and played out an entire scene in his head, imagining what his parents might write to him. In the mornings, he told himself it was foolish and childish to make up such dreams and he really should get on with life and finish editing his article for *Peculiar*.

His article covered everything that had happened in September, which he began as the son of a monster hunter and ended as the parentless partner of an upcoming micro-maze attraction. He described faery hunting with his father, how he had discovered their pet troll was actually the baby son of the sea giants that destroyed San

Francisco (all of *Peculiar*'s readers knew that sea giants were real no matter what the government said), how he was imprisoned by goblins, escaped a giant hoop snake, fought off carnivorous mermaids, and defeated a genuine cynocephaly. He described, too, how his parents were swallowed by a whale. The article ended with an invitation from Bailey to all of *Peculiar*'s readers to come visit Buckleby and Son's Very Strange Souvenirs and to accept a real minotaur's micro-maze challenge, which would open in the spring. If anyone could appreciate a minotaur's labyrinth and the importance of its historical place in Western culture, he knew *Peculiar*'s readers could. All in all, when he had finished writing the piece, he was happy with it, although the story was so packed with monster encounters he feared it might come off as unbelievable. But it couldn't hurt to send it off to the editor. Besides, a publication might look good on his college resume.

By mid-December, when John Muir Middle School had let out for the winter, and Whalefat Beach had grown even more foggy and gray, Bailey began to feel restless and even—somehow—bored. He was running a store and helping his minotaur partner buy building materials. This might have been an unusually interesting life for many seventh graders, but for him it was already becoming quite routine. Was this it? Was it silly and childish to want anything more? Every evening he walked to the beach to look for whales and ratatoskers, but was that a huge waste of time? Because with each passing night, Bailey realized that a reunion with his parents was becoming less and less likely.

Until one Thursday evening when he was sitting behind the cash register and a single envelope slid through the slot of the shop's front door.

CHAPTER FORTY-TWO

THE ANSWER

BAILEY'S HANDS TREMBLED as he opened the letter. He wanted it so badly to be from his parents, telling him they had found their way to a foreign shore and for some reason couldn't call or email or text but could only send him this letter. Who else would send him a letter by snail mail? Only his technologically challenged father. He took a deep breath, unfolded the letter, and read it slowly, one word at a time.

Dear Mr. Bailey Buckleby,

It is my honor to write you. If you are getting this letter, I know the story you submitted to Peculiar is at least partially true. I must admit that even for a seasoned monster hunter like myself, your story seemed fantastical, and because you are a mere twelve years of age, I wondered if you were prone to exaggeration. But when the editor of <u>Peculiar</u> sent me your story, I found it so well written and with such marvelously accurate renditions of North American tunneling goblins, I knew that you were clearly a monster hunter coming into his prime. More than that, the story of your lost parents moved me, and I knew instantly that the gigantic whale that you describe is quite likely the descendant of the great <u>basilosaurus</u>, a dinosaur that my colleagues in paleontology have always suspected still swims our seven oceans. To think that a young man like yourself stood before such a creature! I truly envy your encounter.

Perhaps it is selfish of me to make such a request, but I wonder if you would like to collaborate on another article. The editor of <u>Peculiar</u> is a good friend of mine, and I've already suggested the possibility. He envisions your article as the cover of the January issue and the beginning of an adventure reported in a monthly series as we live it.

Bailey—I say this with no degree of certainty but with utmost hope—I think we may be able to find your parents. I am currently researching and photographing the Eight-Pointed City of the octopeople, which lies beyond a great coral reef just west of Isla Cedros. I know you would find it as fascinating as I do. I wonder if you have plans for the holidays. If not, would you care to join me? You would see no snow on Christmas Day, but the fantastic phosphorescent city of the tentacled octopeople might just make up for it. The octopeople are

well aware of monster traffic beneath the waves and
have told me that a giant whale swims by their city
routinely and is due to come by any day now. I can't help
but wonder, Bailey, if this is the same basilosaurus that
swallowed your mother and father. Perhaps together we
can find the answer you seek. My phone number is 555-246-
8421. Please call me, Bailey. Two monster hunters are
better than one.

Quite sincerely,

Dr. Frederick March

Bailey read the note once more and then again. What
would his father think? His disdain for Dr. March might
be forgotten if he knew he had helped his son earn the
cover story of his favorite magazine.

He packed everything he needed in one backpack—
clothes, Frisbees, and Dr. March's *In the Shadow of Monsters*. He smiled to himself, knowing he would soon be
working with his hero and not just reading his book and
dreaming. He went online and bought a plane ticket to
Mexico. His flight would leave that night.

He gave the keys to the store to Nikos, who was surprised to hear of Bailey's sudden plans but understood
that he had to do what he had to do. He asked Bailey if he
would tell Savannah that he was leaving Whalefat Beach.

"I'll text her," he said. "I won't be gone for long."

Bailey knew that spending winter vacation with Dr.
March would be dangerous and full of monsters, and
finding his parents would be difficult—if not impossible.

But like seven generations of Bucklebys before him, Bailey was a brave monster hunter, so danger and difficulty were not serious considerations. Was it ridiculous to think a scientist he had never met and octopeople he had only read about would be able to help him find the whale that swallowed his parents? Bailey knew his mother would approve when he decided he must follow Dr. March's example, go out into the world, and see for himself.

Acknowledgments

This story could not have been told without my first editor, Julie Scheina, who introduced me to my agent, Sarah Davies, who introduced me to my editor at Macmillan, Julia Sooy. They are three wonderful giants who help put the stars in the sky.